THE **R**ECYCLING OF **R**OSALIE

A NOVEL

PATRICIA MCLAINE

1999
Akasha Publishing
Camden, Maine
USA

1999
Akasha Publishing
Post Office Box 959
Camden, Maine 04843 USA
AkashaCo@aol.com   fax: 207-236-7035

Cover Design: FUSZION | Art + Design
Art Illustrator: Lisa Johnson
Editors: Diana Read and Bita Lanys

ISBN 0-9672510-1-X

Printed in the United States of America in Palatino.

FOR TOMI AND MARK
With Love and Kisses

In Loving Memory of
SUSAN STRASBERG

They have been meeting off and on
for thousands of years
because
LOVE IS ETERNAL.

The Rainbow comes and goes
And lovely is the Rose.

—William Wordsworth
Intimations of Immortality

Chapter One

North Hollywood, California, March 1975

"David's never going to get up on that roof and fix the antenna. He's acrophobic! Hell, I'm a little acrophobic myself, but there he is out selling vacuum cleaners to all those pretty little housewives and here I am stuck in a house with a TV that can't get two or four so that I have to miss my favorite soap opera and all the really decent programs and walk around the stupid house talking to myself. I mean, you can only scrub the floor so often. You can only dust so many times. And you can't sit around and eat all the time when your rear end's already bigger than it should be. So who's going to end up climbing up onto that goddamn roof? Rosalie, that's who! Who else is stupid enough or cares whether I watch two or four?

"David doesn't care. Even if they are the best networks with some of the best shows. David hates television. He calls it a conspiracy against intelligence and creative thinking. Well, if David Rosenberg is so goddamn intelligent and so creative, then what the hell is he doing out there selling vacuum cleaners? I mean, why isn't he the president of the whole goddamn world?"

Rosalie was talking to herself, pacing back and forth. Something she did often. After all, it was supposed to be better to express herself than keep it all in and make herself sick because she was repressed. But then, Rosalie *was* a little repressed. She hadn't even asked David to fix the antenna for a week. Granted, she had asked him to do it several times for several weeks, but David almost never watched television. He couldn't care less about two or four. Maybe it was because he sold vacuum cleaners days, was taking a creative writing class on Tuesday and Thursday nights, and trying to write a book the rest of the time.

Rosalie took a deep breath and sighed as she walked out into the front yard. It helped to relieve her tension as she turned to stare up at the roof. A large black crow was perched on the antenna.

"Get off of there, bird!" she cried out in dismay.

Rosalie shook her short, curly hair. In a fit of depression, she had cut off her long, dark hair last Wednesday afternoon. David had yet to notice. He could be rather unobservant at times. Maybe he needed glasses.

Rosalie narrowed her large, brown eyes, then headed for the open garage. There was a tall wooden ladder against the wall. "What the hell do I know about antennas?" she said to herself as she dragged the ladder to the middle of the driveway where she could better survey the angle of the roof.

After four months, things were beginning to shape up. The house still needed paint on the outside, but Rosalie had already painted three of the rooms. Just that morning she had added orange and yellow poppies to the corners of her kitchen cupboard doors. She planned to add green leaves and stems that afternoon. The landlord would not agree to repaint the neglected house. He thought himself generous in providing the paint for them to fix the inside themselves. It was a small house, nothing to rave about. But it was beginning to feel like home. David hated apartments. Rosalie liked to grow things, flowers in particular. It was hard to grow flowers in an apartment except in boxes and pots. She studied the yard, thinking about the flowers that she would plant that month. Spring was on its way. It was early March.

Still frustrated about missing her favorite soap opera yet one more time, Rosalie decided it might be easier to get up on the roof from the back of the house; she dragged the ladder along.

The backyard wasn't bad. To Rosalie's way of thinking, it just needed lots of flowers and plants. There were no trees, just lots of sun. Rosalie was planning a rose garden. She loved roses. All colors and all sizes. Daisies, too. She wanted pansies and geraniums—lots of pretty colors all around the yard. But for the moment, she stopped mentally landscaping the yard to stare up at the roof. The large crow was still sunning itself on the dilapidated antenna.

"Get off of there, bird! For all I know, it's your fault I can't get two and four!"

With that, the crow flew away, obviously intimidated.

With some effort, she placed the ladder near what she hoped would become their patio. Then she stared up at the roof, reminding herself that it wasn't really that high. It was hardly like climbing a mountain, or even the Statue of Liberty, and yet, she had this strange feeling in the pit of her stomach that crept on up into her chest—a heavy, gnawing sensation that just wouldn't go away. But she did want to see two and four, so up the ladder she went.

The antenna was on the very top of the roof, so she had to climb up to reach it. All the pieces of metal linked together with screws and nuts and bolts looked sort of strange and puzzling. It reminded her of some kind of futuristic scarecrow. Totally put off by the entire situation, she sat down to look over the neighborhood. She had never seen it from the roof before. It looked different. The mail truck was two blocks away. Probably just more bills and advertising, though maybe Honey had sent her a postcard from Miami.

Honey had gone to visit a retired uncle in Florida. She was hoping to meet a tall, dark stranger who would sweep her off her feet and beg her to marry him. She said that was what she saw in her tea leaves. Among other things, Honey MacIntosh read tea leaves. Strange as it seemed to Rosalie, Honey had managed to predict a few things that actually happened, like David changing jobs. But then, no one had been buying encyclopedias. Vacuum cleaners were more in demand. After all, people could go to a library to read an encyclopedia. Everybody needed his or her own vacuum cleaner.

Sometimes Rosalie thought Honey was just a little nutty, but sweet. Really sweet. The name suited her. Honey MacIntosh was Rosalie's best friend. They had known each other for five years, since right after Rosalie had moved from Brooklyn to Los Angeles.

Rosalie noticed two dogs at a standoff at the corner. One lived down the street. The other was a stray. Someday Rosalie wanted a dog of her own. But David didn't want her to get a dog yet. He thought she should go back to work to help out with expenses, so they could save money. Then a dog would have to be left alone, and that wasn't a good idea.

Grocery checker! What an exciting job, standing on her feet all day checking groceries, with everyone complaining about inflation and about how people wouldn't be able to afford to eat anymore, the way things were going. Why didn't people grow their own food and stop buying groceries? That way they could stop complaining. Why did people always gripe and never do anything about changing the things that bothered them?

Rosalie had never realized that climbing up on a roof would make her think about so many different things—like the Goldsmiths' swimming pool south of the boulevard in Encino. Only one of her North Hollywood neighbors had a pool, and it was cracked. It leaked. Someday Rosalie wanted a swimming pool, and maybe a Jacuzzi. Why not? She could wish, couldn't she? It didn't cost her anything to wish.

Why didn't people in the neighborhood take better care of their yards? They rarely even mowed the grass. God forbid they should plant flowers. What a shame. The world definitely looked different from up there. Roofs were obviously a good place to think, even if it could be depressing. Then she remembered the soap opera would be on in an hour, so she turned to glare at the antenna.

"It's too bad you can't talk. Then you could tell me which way to turn you to bring in two and four."

As she stood up to study the metal maze before her, she heard a car pull up in front of the house. David got out. It wasn't his car. He said something she couldn't hear to a driver she couldn't see. He waved as the car sped away. Then David headed for the front door. He hadn't even bothered to look for her on the roof.

"Hey, David!" she called out. "What are you doing home so early?"

David stopped and looked around, puzzled.

"I'm up here, stupid! On the roof! Trying to figure out this goddamn antenna."

David looked up, shading his eyes from the sun, a startled expression on his face. He frowned. He wasn't bad looking. Honey thought he was handsome. But then, Honey was twenty-five, single, overweight, and slightly desperate. David did have beautiful teeth and a nice smile, but according to Rosalie, his ears were too big. They stuck out. And his hair was getting awfully thin for a guy who was only thirty. Besides that, he was skinny. He seldom ate. Rosalie always told him he was lean like Jimmy Stewart, with ears like Clark Gable, and half of Jimmy Durante's nose. No one could miss it right in the middle of that face.

"So what do you think you're doing?" David put his hands on his hips. He was shaking his head and rolling his eyes.

"I told you. I'm fixing the antenna. You may not like television, but I do. And if you won't fix the antenna, then I will. It's as simple as that."

✳

"You're crazy! Do you know that, Rosalie? Plain crazy!" David could feel his blood pressure rising. "I told you that I'd get Kenny to help me with that as soon as I can find the time. I told you that! What do you know about antennas? Nothing! That's what you know. A big fat nothing!"

"So where's the car?" She was beginning to like the roof.

"It caught on fire." He stared into the bushes, his expression flat.

"On fire? What do you mean it caught on fire?"

"The electrical system short-circuited. Something like that." He shrugged it off. "Smoke and flames started pouring out from under the hood and dashboard. The fire department came. It was awful. I had to have the car towed." David was discouraged. "Rosalie, if you want to know the God-honest truth, this has not been one of my favorite days. Not in the least!"

"So what are you going to do now?"

"I don't have a clue what I'm going to do now," he said with a sigh, a strange sensation tugging at his gut. "But I know what you're going to do now. You're going to get down off that stupid roof...that's what you're going to do...before you fall and break your stupid neck!" His voice was tense. After all, David was acrophobic.

"You want to know something, David? I like the roof! Being on a roof is a very interesting experience. You should try it sometime. Really, David, you should try it!"

She knew she was being ridiculous but she couldn't care less. So now the car had caught on fire. What next? How could David sell vacuum cleaners without a car? He couldn't carry all that stuff around from door to door, and they did have to pay the rent.

"Rosalie, will you please get off of that roof? You're making me nervous. Please!" he screamed. Now he was pacing. Next, his ulcer would start giving him trouble.

That was when a strange thing happened. The big black crow that had been sitting on the power lines suddenly flew off and took a dive straight at Rosalie. As she dodged to one side to get out of its way, she lost her balance, fell, and started rolling down the front of the roof. She was so startled by what had happened that she didn't even cry out. The last thing she was aware of as she fell headfirst toward the front porch was David running toward her crying out, "R o s a l i e!" at the top of his voice. ✣

Chapter Two

All around there was a bright golden mist—sort of like fog but it wasn't cold and damp and it wasn't hot. It was pleasant. Rosalie could hear music. Not ordinary music. More like harmonious notes accompanied by a choir of perfectly blended voices. Something indescribable. Nothing she had ever heard before could even begin to compare with it.

She had a warm, lazy, drifting sensation, like floating in the Goldsmiths' swimming pool with the temperature at eighty-eight degrees, or lying in a warm bathtub full of bubbles. There was a sweet fragrance that reminded her of spring flowers after rain combined with the scent of freshly mowed grass. And just as she was beginning to adapt to the mist, strange light, and lovely sensations, she discovered she actually was resting on freshly mowed grass. There were beautiful, brilliant flowers all around her. Flowers she could not remember ever having seen before.

"Now why can't my yard look like this?" As usual, Rosalie was talking to herself.

The mist was clearing. About a hundred yards away a wide, calm, deep blue river flowed. All around in the distance there were gentle rolling hills, lush and green. Rosalie was entranced as an orange and white and blue butterfly alit nearby. She was especially fond of butterflies, and had never seen this kind before.

"You're beautiful."

Rosalie talked to butterflies the same as she talked to flowers and plants and to herself.

To her utter delight, the butterfly fluttered up and settled on her knee. Once when she was a small child, a brown and yellow butterfly with bright blue dots on its wings had stayed on her hand for several minutes. It was one of her fondest memories. The same as then, she was afraid to move or say anything, afraid if she did that the butterfly might fly away. Nonetheless, the butterfly stayed on her knee, gently moving its wings in the soft breeze.

Slowly, Rosalie sat up, took a deep breath, and gazed at the magnificent landscape all around her. The butterfly was still there on her knee. She wondered if it thought the bright green pants she was wearing were an extension of the grass. Then it suddenly fluttered up in front of her face, navigating a change of course toward the river. Rosalie watched, sitting very still, filled with an extraordinary sense of well-being.

Then, as though from out of nowhere, a rowboat appeared on the river. The man rowing the boat was dressed in black and wore a clerical collar. He had a Santa Claus sort of face without a beard, and as he rowed he heartily sang out, "Row, row, row your boat, gently down the stream...Merrily, merrily, merrily, merrily, life is but a dream...Row, row, row your boat gently down the stream...." What he lacked in voice, he made up for in enthusiasm.

Then the man got out of the boat at a small pier near the edge of the river and waved. Rosalie looked all around her. Since she was the only one there, she waved back. He looked harmless enough. He was all smiles. He walked toward her at a quick pace for such an old gent.

"Hello, hello! And how are you this fine moment?" His voice had a lilt that was Irish.

Rosalie tilted her head to one side, the way she always did when she was trying to figure someone out. "I'm fine," she replied. "Just fine."

"I'm so very glad to hear that." And with that, he sat down to join her on the grass. "Lovely here, isn't it? I particularly like this spot."

"Yes, it's beautiful."

It was at that moment she realized that she had absolutely no idea of where she was or of how she had even gotten there. Strange, Rosalie thought, and began to search her mind.

"Excuse me," she finally said, "but for some strange reason I don't seem to remember..." she stopped short and cautiously inquired, "That is, could you possibly tell me...where we are?"

"Most folks call it Halfway Point here near the crossing. It has other names, of course, depending on your point of view. I like Halfway Point. It's a descriptive name and quite accurate."

Rosalie was still puzzled, but for the moment she felt so good about being there she guessed it didn't matter much how she had really gotten there, and yet, "What river is that?" she decided to ask.

"Before we discuss the river, allow me to introduce myself. I'm Father Timothy." As he spoke he pulled a piece of paper out of his jacket pocket. "Naturally, I already know your name. Rosalie...Rosalie Rosenberg."

"How come you know my name? Are you psychic or something?"

"You could say that," he replied with a chuckle. "But actually, your name was given to me by my superior."

"What superior?" Things were getting stranger by the minute.

"Well, I call her Mother Superior," he was chuckling again. "It's a little private joke we have between us. But most people here call her Marcella. You'll like her. She's a wonderful being." He neatly folded the paper and put it back into his pocket.

Rosalie was searching her mind, trying to remember how she had gotten to this place. Nothing was making sense. How could this Marcella person know her name when she couldn't remember ever having met anyone named Marcella at any time or any place in her entire life? And even if she had, why would Marcella give her name to this odd little guy in a black suit? And how did he know she would even be here in the first place, wherever *here* was? There was something very strange going on.

"Are we anywhere near Los Angeles?" she ventured to ask.

"Dimensionally speaking," Father Timothy replied, "you could say that, and yet, we're not really anywhere near Los Angeles at all." He thoughtfully closed his eyes for a moment.

Rosalie braced herself, her voice tense as she asked, "Then where are we?"

Again, Father Timothy momentarily closed his eyes. There was a long pause before he opened them to look directly into hers. He was searching for the right words, a pensive expression on his face. "What's the last thing that you remember, lass?"

"Asking you where we are." Now, she was really getting nervous.

"No, I mean..."

"Before what?" she blurted out. "What I mean is, what do you mean by before?"

"Before you found yourself here?"

"Before I found myself here?" she more or less squeaked as she scratched her head. Not that it itched. It was something she frequently did when she was nervous. "That's one hell of a question. I mean, just a few minutes ago, I was trying to figure out where I am and how I got here, and now you're asking me to remember."

She frowned before continuing, "If you want to know the truth, I seem to have amnesia or something, like I don't remember. Honest, I just plain don't remember." With that she let out a long sigh, then got up and looked around as though the flowers and trees would fill her in. "This is the weirdest thing that's ever happened to me. Honest. I'm not putting you on. Honest, I'm not. I don't know where I am. I know who I am. I'm Rosalie Rosenberg—just like your friend Marcella, or Mother Superior, or whatever you two have going on, says."

He raised a mildly disapproving eyebrow.

"No offense intended," she quickly added, again scratching her head. "And if you want to know something really strange, for some crazy reason I don't even give a shit!"

At the word *shit* Father Timothy closed his eyes for a full ten seconds, then released a softly controlled sigh.

"I'm sorry. I guess my choice of words isn't always the greatest," she said with a grin. "I mean, you must be a rabbi or something, and I guess religious folk aren't too keen on hearing obscene language, so I apologize. I'm truly sorry." She sounded sincere enough.

"I accept your apology." Father Timothy took a deep breath and squared his shoulders before saying, "It's not uncommon for people to feel as you do when they first arrive. The truth is, many do. Some at least remember that they were on their way, but in your case, I guess there wasn't time to prepare for the transition."

"Transition?" Again Rosalie scratched her head.

"My dear Rosalie, you have crossed over."

"Crossed over where?"

"To the other side."

"The other side of what?" her voice was rising in pitch, the way it always did when she was really nervous. "Los Angeles?"

He simply shook his head, a somewhat strained expression on his face.

"California?"

Again he shook his head.

"The world?"

"Not exactly," he replied, then paused for a moment. "But then, I suppose you could say that." He was aware of her plight, having dealt with many such souls before. Recently, they were becoming his specialty.

Rosalie was about to panic. "Well, since your friend Marcella knows who I am, and that I was going to be here, maybe we should ask her how I got here. I mean, I'm sure she'll be able to clear everything up for both of us in nothing flat." For all she knew, this guy was some kind of nut case that had just escaped from the state mental ward at Camarillo.

"I really wish they wouldn't give me these assignments," he said half to himself.

"I'm an assignment? Sure, that makes a lot of sense."

"We have jobs here. The same as you do there. Tasks to help us grow. The jobs we have here can be just as trying as the ones you have on the earth plane. Believe me."

"Earth plane?"

"That's correct, earth plane."

"Oh, come on," she started to laugh, "you're not going to tell me that I'm on Mars or something? I mean, I'll admit I've never seen butterflies like that before, but I haven't been to a lot of places. For all I know, those butterflies are common in Africa or the Amazon or someplace like that. And I know I've never seen flowers like those before, but I've only been in New York, New Jersey, and California. I haven't been to a lot of places that have all kinds of strange things that most people only see in pictures—or those nature programs on TV. Am I dreaming or something? Am I having some kind of freaky dream where I can't wake up? Maybe I've lost my marbles. Maybe I'm hallucinating because some stupid doper put LSD in the drinking water." Her head was reeling at the implications.

"Come on, Timothy, level with me. You're not trying to tell me what I think you're trying to tell me, are you? I mean, the last thing I can remember is trying to figure out the goddamn antenna. Then David drove up, and this stupid crow took a dive at me so that I lost my balance and fell and rolled down the roof and..." she stopped cold, raising both hands to her face.

"Go on," Father Timothy said, an understanding look on his face.

Rosalie took a deep breath and let it out slowly. Her voice was barely above a whisper when she said, "What you're trying to tell me is…I'm dead. That Rosalie Rosenberg has died."

He nodded without saying a word. She had finally accepted the truth. 🐝

Chapter Three

"But I don't feel dead! Not the least bit dead!" she was shouting and slapping her thigh. "You can't tell me that's spirit. I've got a body. A real body!"

"You needn't shout!" Father Timothy replied as Rosalie proceeded to give him a tentative nudge.

"And you're no spirit either! You see there!" She looked so relieved. "I just know that any minute now David is going to wake me up and tell me to scramble him three eggs, not too runny, and make it fast." She hugged herself, rubbing her hands over her arms for reinforcement, then opened her eyes, blinking twice before staring straight at him. "How can I be dead when I feel better than I ever felt in my life? I mean, I feel terrific!"

"Naturally. Here most people feel better than they ever felt in their lives. Not that we don't have our fair share of problems. We just no longer have a gross physical vehicle to suffer the aches and pains of mortality. That experience is reserved for the earth plane."

"What do you mean gross physical vehicle?" She reached over to pinch him. "You have a body. I can feel it. I touched you!"

"Naturally! Once you get here the body you have here seems just as tangible as the body you had there seemed when you were there, if I'm making myself clear. You just vibrate at a different frequency. And this body isn't the last word in otherworldly fashions—take my word for it."

"This is all so crazy, it just doesn't make sense. So how did I die?"

"Rather abruptly."

"Just like that, huh?" she snapped her fingers, hardly amused by her state of affairs.

"You could say that. It's a blessing really, crossing over quickly. The only difficulty can be the temporary shock to the psyche. It's not uncommon to find such souls totally unaware of their transition, as in your case."

"That's just great!" Rosalie exclaimed, then sighed. Her friend Honey had taught her to sigh to relieve nervous tension. If she didn't have a physical body, she wondered why she felt so tense about finding out that she was dead.

"It's quite simple," Father Timothy began, "nervous tension is totally psychological—a creation of the mind. Here we're all mind. On earth we were really all mind, too, but there it isn't nearly as apparent as it soon becomes in this dimension."

Rosalie stared at him in disbelief. Had she been thinking out loud?

"I didn't ask you anything. I didn't ask you to explain anything!" What a freaky place this was turning out to be. Dead or whatever, she wasn't quite prepared for this guy.

"I'm terribly sorry." He was upset with himself. "I'll probably get chastised good for that one. We're supposed to pace ourselves with the new arrivals, not throw them into a quandary. It seems like I've been on these assignments forever, but my judgment is obviously still in further need of refinement. Please forgive me. I did not intend in any way to upset you."

"You were reading my mind—is that it?" Rosalie's mood softened.

He was relieved that she wasn't angry and went on to explain, "It's common here, and even more so higher up.

You'll be able to do it yourself in no time at all. Thoughts aren't really private on earth either, regardless of what some people may think. Everything is recorded, seen and heard by those destined to know. An unnerving discovery initially, but it does help souls to shape up rather quickly."

"I can see where it would." She half-smiled, wistfully surveying the scenery around her.

"Halfway Point, huh?" Her eyes followed the course of the river. "Does that mean I'm halfway to heaven or halfway to hell? I mean, I've never been a religious person. I haven't gone to temple since I don't know when. It isn't that I don't believe in God. It's just that I've never thought much about things like this. I've never thought much at all about dying. You see, I'm only twenty-nine."

"I know."

"If I'd known I was going to die at twenty-nine, I wouldn't have worried so much about turning thirty. It really bothered me a lot the past few years." She suddenly began pacing; taking everything in and trying to digest it was not proving an easy task. She abruptly turned to face him.

"Did I fall and break my neck, or what?" Her voice was filled with tension.

"I'm afraid so, lass," he said in sincere sympathy.

"Well, then I hope to hell I'm on the welcoming committee when that goddamn crow makes his transition!" Now she was shouting, "In fact, I hope he gets torn to pieces by an eagle or some kind of vulture. I never have been crazy about crows. Now I have no use for them whatsoever."

"Vengeance is mine sayeth the Lord!" Father Timothy was not smiling.

"Like hell you say! How would you like to be done in by some stupid blackbird that has been screwing up your TV antenna? That stupid crow murdered me!"

Father Timothy grimaced, bracing himself for the onslaught.

"How would you like to die by falling off a stupid one-story house because your stupid husband nearly faints if he has to stand on a chair to change a light bulb? David's so acrophobic he couldn't possibly climb up on the roof to fix the antenna so that I could get two and four and not be bored to death sitting around the stupid house doing absolutely nothing after I've painted and cleaned and done everything else I could think of." Her emotions were building to a fever pitch. "And I even had to put the trash out on Tuesday mornings because David always forgot on Monday nights!" Now she was crying.

"Busy man, David Rosenberg. I cut off my stupid hair and he didn't even notice—six inches! If I cut off my head, he probably still wouldn't notice."

"Take three deep breaths and count to ten," Father Timothy was tuning into her distress. "Your energy field is rapidly becoming depleted by...."

"I don't give a damn about my energy field!" She was crying and walking in circles, distraught and disoriented. "I didn't even live to be thirty. I'll never believe one of those goddamn horoscope magazines again as long as I live!" The tears freely flowed, coursing down both cheeks. "If this is supposed to be a good year for Aquarians, what in the hell is a bad year going to be like?"

Father Timothy handed her a large white handkerchief.

"Watch out, Aquarians! No roof climbing this year or the goddamn birds will get you—just like they did in that rerun last week on channel eleven. Jesus!"

At that point Timothy wanted to disappear but thought better of it. Mother Superior wouldn't be all that pleased. Instead, he patiently waited for the storm to pass as Rosalie threw herself down on the grass, sobbing her heart out.

"If I'm dead, why can I cry real tears?"

"That isn't the easiest thing to explain, lass." he said as he sat down facing her, revving up his heart center for all he was worth, projecting as much love and comfort as he could possibly muster. He had never before been assigned to a new arrival anything like Rosalie. "I guess I should have brought along a helper," he half said to himself.

"So go find yourself a helper!" The sobs lessened. "Who in the hell are you, anyway?" She blew her nose into the handkerchief.

"I told you," he was a bit flustered. "I'm Father Timothy."

"Isn't that what they call Catholic priests? Father?"

He simply nodded.

"Well, I'm no Catholic. I'm Jewish. And I'm not even a religious Jew. Is this what happens to non-religious Jews when they die? Some Catholic priest comes to take them to hell in a rowboat?" Once again she blew her nose.

He could only smile. "No, lass." He gently took her hand in his. "I've not come to take you to hell in a rowboat." He took a deep breath and sighed. Honey's advice for relieving nervous tension was a very old remedy. Timeless, in fact. "The reason I still dress in this fashion is because I was a priest in my last incarnation."

"Your what?"

"Earth life." The look on his face was fatherly, tender. "You see, when I was last on earth I was in the priesthood, and sometimes I find it helpful to maintain that image. This is obviously not one of those times."

"Obviously." She tried to smile.

"The adjustments never end, you know. There's always something more to learn." He was so relieved that the storm had passed. "And lately, they've been giving me mainly problem cases."

"I'm not surprised to hear you say that." Rosalie sat up, tears again filling her eyes. "Some people thought I was a problem when I was alive." Once again, Rosalie was crying.

"I didn't mean to suggest..." he stammered.

"Now that I'm dead, I guess I'm still a problem! That's just terrific!" She was trying not to cry. "My friend, Honey MacIntosh, always said that all our problems end when we die, but that doesn't seem to be the case, does it? She always said that the only people who end up in real serious trouble are the murderers and the ones who commit suicide. Is that true?"

"Well, suicides do get such a shock. I mean, they thought they were going to end it all, only to discover there's no ending. They still have to face all their problems, and there's a far greater chance of making things worse than there is of making things better. But then, most souls tend to discover the truth too late. Poor things. Murderers have to pay for what they've done in a multitude of manners. It is never a good thing to take a life—your own or anyone else's. It runs contrary to Universal Law."

"So what you're telling me is—there is no death."

"You're a quick study, lass," he responded, giving her an affectionate pat. "We're going to get on just fine."

Rosalie studied him a moment before turning to gaze at the river. "Is that the River Styx?"

"For some. For others it's the Jordan. The river has different meanings for each soul."

For a moment they both just stood there and watched the mighty, flowing river as brightly colored butterflies fluttered near its banks where wispy, weeping willow branches dipped slender leaves into the refreshing, clear water.

"What do you call the river?" she asked him.

"I call it the River of Consciousness." His expression was pensive. "Marcella calls it the River of Life. Consciousness is life and life is consciousness, so it seems we're both right."

"Would it be all right if I just call you Timothy? You're not my father."

"You may call me anything you like," he quickly added, "within reason."

"Timothy's a nice name. What's your last name?"

"O'Toole."

"Timothy O'Toole! That sounds like something straight out of an old Bing Crosby movie. Come to think of it, you look like someone straight out of an old Bing Crosby movie."

Timothy had heard the comment more than once. He accepted it as some sort of compliment, although he had never seen a Bing Crosby movie.

Rosalie and Timothy continued to stand side by side watching the river, watching butterflies and birds and bees, majestic trees, and all the pretty flowers growing in abundance as far as the eye could see. It seemed like hours had passed since Rosalie had found herself in this special place; yet the same golden glow filled the wide expanse of the sky all around them. Everything appeared to stay the same. There was a sense of constancy. This place was more beautiful than any place she had ever before seen or imagined. An indescribable peace filled her entire being.

So this is what it's like when you die, she thought. You come to a beautiful place with grass and flowers and butterflies and trees and a peaceful, gently flowing river—a place with open meadows and rolling hills. Nice, she thought. But is this all there is?

"What do we do next? I mean, don't get me wrong, I love rivers and flowers and all this nature stuff, but is this all there is to do around here?"

"Not at all. There is much to do around here." His face lit up as he spoke, "I guess it's time we get you settled in."

"Settled in? What do you mean?"

He carefully took a folded piece of paper out of his pocket and studied it, "Well, it says here: spacious colonial facing the lake, canopy bed and fireplace in master bedroom, lovely garden, den with fireplace and recliner, and a television in every room with excellent reception." He smiled a Santa Claus sort of smile. "How does that sound?"

"Like a real estate ad in the *Valley Times*." He had just described her dream house. "No swimming pool?"

"I seem to have overlooked the pool and the Jacuzzi, whatever that might be."

"Are you putting me on?" She could hardly believe her ears.

"Did I leave anything else out?" Timothy always liked this part best.

"Are you kidding?" She started jumping up and down; then she grabbed his hand and started pulling him along.

"Come on. What are we waiting for? I'm dying to see it!"

"You'd be amazed how often I hear those very words. Ironic, wouldn't you say?"

"Yeah, sure! Well, I did, didn't I? I had to die and go to heaven to get my dream house. Fall off of a goddamn roof and break my stupid neck just like David was afraid I would. If that isn't a crock!" Now she was laughing. "So where is this wonderful, glorious place?"

"Not far, dimensionally speaking," he said, a smile on his face, though he certainly hoped she would soon stop saying *goddamn*.

"I guess they have to do something nice for you when you get here to make up for what you went through when you were down there. I mean, it seems logical. Right?"

"I suppose you could call it logical." There was a faraway look in his eyes as they walked toward the pier at the edge of the river.

"A television set in every room," she said, shaking her head, "I'll be goddamned!"

Timothy blanched and rolled his eyes, then took a deep breath and slowly exhaled as they continued walking toward the river.

"Are the programs any good around here? I mean, what are they like?"

"If you'll pardon the expression," he said with smiling eyes, "they're divine." ✳

Chapter Four

The strangest thing happened when they reached the edge of the river. A thick golden mist suddenly enveloped both of them. The very next moment they were walking down a shady, tree-lined street without any sidewalks, similar to one Rosalie remembered in Encino. The houses were all upper-middle-class with very nice yards. Here and there people went about the business of the day. Two children riding bicycles passed them, waving as they rode by.

"Friends of yours?" Rosalie was dazed by the sudden turn of events.

"Everyone is friendly here. The disagreeable ones seek their own level." He appeared to be checking addresses.

"I'm not going to ask you how we got here," she admitted, forcing herself to deal with one thing at a time. "I mean, it's just the kind of neighborhood I've always wanted to live in, but David was only a vacuum cleaner salesman, and they don't clean up that much, if you get my meaning." She laughed at her own pun.

Timothy simply smiled good-naturedly. Vacuum cleaners had not been a part of his experience.

Two magnificent Persian cats romped on a lawn in front of a grand English Tudor home. If she didn't know better, Rosalie would swear she was somewhere in Encino or maybe, Chatham, New Jersey. How very strange, she thought.

They stopped in front of a grand, two-story, white colonial with a large, perfectly green lawn. Along the front of the house a variety of colorful flowers bloomed in profusion. White daisy bushes flanked the stairs leading to the porch with its two tall white columns. Plants of every size and variety grew everywhere. On one side of the yard a large ornamental cherry tree was covered with bright pink blossoms. It was gorgeous. Across from the house was a large, crystal-blue lake where a young couple strolled hand in hand. Out in the distance, two boats in full white sail glided in unison through the water. It was picture-perfect.

When Rosalie turned to him, Father Timothy had a broad smile on his face.

"I trust you find the neighborhood to your liking? You can see the lake from most of the rooms. We thought the setting might help you to meditate."

"If meditating is anything like thinking, you're right."

Just seeing the lake stirred a childhood memory. Rosalie remembered going to a similar lake in upstate New York when she was still a child—a lake surrounded by tall trees with birds singing in their branches and lots of bushy gray squirrels running all about. She had tried fishing there, but rarely caught fish. She would sit there, patiently waiting, thinking and thinking. It helped her solve some of her problems. When she saw the look on Timothy's face, she knew he had been reading her mind again.

Come to think of it, there had been a house on that lake, too. Hardly as grand as this one, though there had been times when she had wished and wondered what it would be like to live in a house beside a lake some day. As she looked into Timothy's blue eyes, she wondered just how much he really knew about her.

"Not nearly enough," he quickly replied. "I'm looking forward to learning much, much more."

"Oh, yeah?" She was right. He was doing it again. She narrowed her eyes before saying, "Well, if you can read my mind all the time, I guess I don't need to tell you anything."

"On the contrary," Timothy protested, "we have a strict code of ethics here. No prying allowed." With that he started walking up the brick walk toward the house. "I suppose you'd like to see what you've created."

Rosalie didn't answer. She took off running, calling over her shoulder, "I suppose you have the key."

"You'll be needing no keys here, lass. Just make yourself at home."

With the anticipation of a small child on Christmas morning, she flung the large double doors open wide and was not disappointed by what met her eyes.

The rich hardwood floors of the entry were partially covered by a stunning oriental carpet with a mandala design in peach and green and blue and beige. Tall, sweeping potted palms stood on either side. It was absolutely perfect. A magnificent crystal chandelier suspended from a two-story ceiling near the top of an impressive winding staircase glistened in the light.

In the living room with its grand marble fireplace were fine antiques in cherry and mahogany, and elegant sofas and chairs upholstered in bright floral chintz in her favorite spring colors. Everything was exquisite. Tiffany lamps. Bronze statues. Delicate porcelain figurines. Hand-painted Chinese vases. Lush green plants and potted trees added just the right touches near the windows. Crystal vases spilled over with gorgeous floral arrangements. In her vivid imagination Rosalie had created the setting, the house, all of it. It was everything she had ever dreamed and hoped and yearned and wished and wanted it to be, down to the very last tassel.

Her dream kitchen was adorned with blue and white gingerbread decor. Copper pots and pans dangled from the ceiling and walls. Assorted apothecary jars on the counters were filled with spices, herbs, cookies, and teas. There was even an antique coffee mill like the one Aunt Sarah had promised to leave her in her will. Rosalie briefly wondered whom Aunt Sarah would leave it to now.

In the dining room was a hand-carved antique oak table with matching chairs upholstered with green velvet. Bright yellow roses in Waterford crystal adorned the center of the table beside a silver candelabrum. The oak breakfront exhibited delicate hand-painted china in her favorite design, as well as cut-crystal goblets and decanters and brightly polished silver trays. For Rosalie, this was truly heaven.

Outside the French doors of the living room was a brick patio filled with flowers and plants. Rosalie ran out into the backyard to see the swimming pool, which was designed like a natural pond. Ferns and a variety of orchids encircled the waterfall at the deep end. Tropical birds were singing high up in a banana tree—the fulfillment of yet another dream.

The weeping willow tree had a special swing, and the rose garden was glorious. There was every color, size, and shape of rose imaginable—as well as some Rosalie had never imagined. Flowers were everywhere, all types and kinds. She joyously ran from one to the other, inhaling their sweet fragrance and blessing every one. Everything was beautiful. Wonderful. Perfect. Then she turned to find a patch of freshly cultivated soil.

"What goes in here?" she asked, turning to find Timothy stretched out in the hammock.

"We thought we'd leave that up to you. Hear tell you enjoy gardening."

Rosalie could hardly contain herself. "Oh, my God! I'll have to think about it later. Right now, I can't think at all. It's all so perfect, so wonderful. I can hardly believe I'm really here—that all of this is really mine. All mine."

Father Timothy simply smiled and attempted to nod from his prone position in the swaying hammock. He always enjoyed the time of discovery for those in his charge.

"The bedroom! I haven't seen the bedroom." With that she turned and ran back into the house and up the winding stairs, taking two steps at a time.

The bathroom had a sunken marble Jacuzzi tub with a skylight overhead, brilliant sunlight streaming into the room. There were Italian tiles just like the ones in the January issue of *House Beautiful* she had saved for over three years—lavender and French blue with a touch of pink. Delicate crystal and china bottles adorned the antique dressing table with its gold-leafed mirror that was fit for a queen.

But the bedroom was the crowning glory. The brass canopy bed, draped in yellow organza and emerald green velvet, had a multitude of prissy pillows propped this way and that. There was a golden marble heart-shaped fireplace with cupids posed with arrows on an ornate brass screen. Tiffany lamps. Vases from the Renaissance. Oil paintings by European masters. And a finely crafted cherry armoire along one wall.

Rosalie leaped into the middle of the bed, curling up on her emerald-green tufted bedspread amongst dainty white lace pillows. She placed a heart-shaped pillow behind her head; then she gingerly pinched herself to make sure it was all truly happening. That was when Father Timothy appeared at her bedroom door.

"Isn't this the most beautiful bedroom you have ever seen in your entire life?" she sang out as she hugged herself tight.

"First-class, I'd say."

"Really first-class. So this is heaven," she said with a sigh, leaning back against the cushions, "I'll be damned!"

Timothy winced before carefully stating, "Let's just say that you have taken a definite step up. There is yet, however, a whole lot further to go."

"You mean I'm not in heaven?"

"A pig wallowing in the mud is in heaven. A bird flying on the wing is in heaven. Heaven's not a place, lass. It's a state of mind. It's all really rather relative."

"A cold-water flat on the seventh floor with no elevator in Brooklyn, New York, isn't heaven. A cockroach in the kitchen isn't heaven. A toilet that won't flush isn't heaven. And a TV that won't get two and four isn't heaven either. Trust me, I know." She snuggled into the pillows. "But this, this is heaven."

The moment he looked as though he might say something in further protest, she held up one hand, "Look, I'll take your word for it. I'll think about it later. Right now, I can't think. Today has been a lulu, as my Aunt Beatrice would say. I had no idea that dying would be anything like this. I mean, I know people, who if they knew, would kill themselves just to get here. My God! All your fondest dreams come true the day you wake up dead. I mean, it's like having strawberry shortcake for breakfast, when you were expecting oatmeal. Being dead is terrific, especially when being dead isn't really being dead at all." She finally stopped talking, waiting for him to say something.

"Aren't you going to say anything?"

"There are times when one learns more by listening to oneself than by hearing what others have to say. Have you been listening to yourself, lass?"

"Not really. But I have instant recall so I can play it all back later." She closed her eyes. "Right now, this very moment, I just want to take this all in. For all I know, I could still wake up in my bed back home and discover that I never climbed up on that roof in the first place so I could fall off it and die in the second place. Maybe I'm just having a crazy, wild, wonderful dream."

Again she closed her eyes, then carefully opened just one to find out if everything around her would still be the same. It was all still there.

"Life is but a dream," Timothy wistfully commented.

Rosalie sat forward, wide-eyed. "Well, if that's the case, life can also be a nightmare." She scanned the room and asked him, "So where's the TV?"

Timothy nodded toward the armoire.

Rosalie leapt from the bed to open the doors of the armoire wide. "Wow! I've never seen one this big before. Is it color?" She began searching for the controls. "How do you turn this set on?"

"It will come on at the appropriate time."

"You mean you only get programs at certain times here?"

"You could say that. A curious invention, television. The world has changed a great deal since the last time I was there."

Father Timothy walked over to the window to look out at the lake. "You have a wonderful view of the lake from here."

Rosalie was still checking out the television set—no switches, dials, or cords anywhere in sight. "This set isn't even connected. Don't tell me that I have to call a TV repairman right off the bat?" she was shaking her head in disgust. "One thing I can tell you for damn sure—I'm not climbing up on any roof. Once was enough."

"That won't be necessary. Since we exist within the Source, there is no need for wires—and since consciousness is the real tuning device, there is no need for switches."

"How about a *TV Guide*? Do you have one of those?"

Timothy smiled and shook his head before turning to gaze out the window.

"How the hell am I supposed to know what to watch when or what time?" Rosalie was beginning to sulk like a child.

"Come to think of it, what time is it, anyway? I haven't seen any clocks around here." She looked around the room—no clock in sight. Back in North Hollywood she had a clock in every room. For the past couple of years Rosalie had developed a sort of fetish concerning time.

"Time is an illusion of earthly existence. You now exist in eternity. And actually, you always have."

"Great! For clock-watchers coming here must be pure hell."

"Only for a period of time," Timothy said with a chuckle.

"Will you please make up your mind." She threw a pillow at him, which he aptly caught.

"Infinite existence is a difficult concept for many mortals to grasp. On all planes of existence there can be constant need for adjustment. We have to keep stretching, expanding our awareness further and further. It's an endless process, but terribly exciting, since the very reason for existence keeps taking on wondrous new meaning, and even startling dimensions. Clock-watchers eventually adjust to the concept of infinite existence just like everyone else. Actually, there's a sort of time for most of us here at this level, a continuity of happenings that appears to start in one place and end in another. So you can see that time is a very difficult concept to surrender."

"Yeah!" was all she could think of saying.

She could understand some of what he was saying and figured she had eternity to come to terms with it. So rather than ask further questions, she got up and joined him at the window. Sailboats were no longer in sight. The sun appeared to be setting. An incandescence of pink, lavender, purple, and pale gray filled the sky over the trees, casting a silver shimmer on the surface of the lake. It was beginning to resemble a giant mirror.

"How can there be sunsets without time?" she felt the need to ask.

"Many things are difficult to explain here as well as on earth," Father Timothy replied, as he watched the fading splendor before them. "My best explanation would be that each of us creates our own reality. It is desire that creates manifestation. Whatever holds meaning for you in your heart becomes a part of you forever, like the beauty of a sunset."

He could see that she was growing weary. "Perhaps the time has come for you to rest."

Rosalie yawned as the sun sank below the tall, towering trees. When she turned to him she planted a brief kiss on his pink cheek. "You're really sweet. Do you know that?"

Timothy blushed.

"I never knew my grandparents. They all died before I was born. I always wanted a grandfather just like my friend

Peggy's. You sort of remind me of him. She was Irish, too. Maybe she was one of your descendants."

"Priests are not allowed to marry," Timothy assured her.

"Do they ever fool around a little?" she asked with a silly grin.

Timothy indignantly shook his head.

"Too bad," she retorted. "You missed out on one hell of a good time."

Timothy blushed, at a loss for words. It would obviously take time for his energy field to adjust to Rosalie's level of awareness.

"On the other hand, I guess you can't miss what you've never had. I mean, let's face it. There are other things in life besides sex."

That was when she noticed the closet door ajar, and decided to take a look inside. To her amazement, the large walk-in closet was filled with an assortment of fashionable clothes in just her size. She immediately found a filmy yellow nightgown and ran out to hold it up in front of herself in front of the large cheval mirror.

"Hey, you guys think of everything! Is this gorgeous or what!"

She twirled around the room holding the nightgown up in front of her.

"I've always wanted a nightgown like this. In fact, I used to do a lot of floor shopping at Holly's Harp. Little did I know I'd have to join the angels to get the stuff for my very own."

"Floor shopping?" Timothy did not understand.

"Walking around the floor pretending that you're shopping. You say to yourself, in your mind, of course, I'll take one of these and one of those, and throw in one of them as well." Rosalie mimed it out while Timothy observed.

"That way you go home with lots of imaginary packages with imaginary clothes inside you can only wear in your imagination. Imagination I had. Money I didn't. Sometimes it was fun pretending. Other times it was depressing, because I always knew I'd never be able to buy the clothes for real."

Rosalie returned to the closet to check out some of the other clothes.

"It couldn't be better if I'd done the shopping myself." She pulled a white bathrobe with gold embroidery off a hanger and stared hard at it. "This is really strange. I mean, I imaginarily bought this bathrobe about a month ago." She searched for the designer's label.

"We don't label things here, lass. They all come from the same Source."

"Next you'll be telling me that God made my bathrobe," she flippantly replied.

"Aye, you could say that now."

She eyed him suspiciously. "Well then, tell Him that He has excellent taste."

"You just told Him yourself," he replied, trying to suppress a silly grin.

"What do you mean? Is this place tapped?"

"My dear Rosalie, the entire universe is tapped."

"Invasion of privacy, huh? Big Daddy has to know it all."

Timothy cleared his throat and explained, "Divine Mind is all-pervading."

"Some of the things you're telling me don't make me feel secure, in case you'd like to know. I mean, first you read my mind. Now, you're telling me that Divine Mind is listening to everything I say. You want to know something? I'm beginning to feel paranoid," Rosalie began to pace. "I mean, you really have to watch your step around here."

"It's like that on earth as well," his tone was gently matter-of-fact.

"Oh, yeah!" She did not find his words reassuring. "Well, maybe it is, and maybe you're just trying to scare the hell out of me. All I know is, I didn't know about it there, and what you don't know can't make you feel paranoid. People were beginning to talk about ESP, things like that. But anybody I ever knew that was into it was suspect—like Honey with her tea leaves and talk about past lives. She said she was a gypsy in a former life—that was why she could read people's fortunes in their tea leaves. Meshuga!"

"Is that a fact now?" A mysterious smile formed on Timothy's lips.

"Hey! What day is this, anyway?"

"It's difficult to say."

"Well, what day did I die?" She thought hard for a moment. "I know, it was Tuesday, and it was March." She rolled her eyes and her face went pale. "March the fifteenth. It was the fifteenth of March!" She stood very still, incredulously shaking her head; then she got goose bumps all over and shivered. "I'll be goddamned!" Rosalie closed her eyes for a long moment.

"I do wish you wouldn't use that phrase," Timothy protested with a grimace.

"Jesus Christ!" she then exclaimed, giving his energy field an even larger jolt. "I know this is going to sound really weird, but the last time Honey read my tea leaves, she made some weird crack like *Beware the ides of March and raven's wings!*" Again Rosalie shivered. "Like she was doing Shakespeare, and quoting—*Macbeth* or something."

"*Julius Caesar*," he flatly corrected.

"That doesn't make me feel any better!" Again she shivered, large goose bumps running up and down her arms and back that crept up onto her scalp. She rubbed her arms to warm herself, hugging herself tightly. "What a coincidence! I'm sure she said raven's wings, and all I could think of at the time was that she was stealing lines from Shakespeare and Edgar Allen Poe at the same crack."

"It seems your friend Honey is somewhat intuitive," Timothy said, watching her closely.

"Well, if she's so intuitive, why didn't she just tell me not to climb on roofs with crows on power lines during the month of March? I mean, what's with the poetry and raven's wings bit? Why didn't she just say that I could fall off a roof and break my goddamn neck? She could at least have said crow's wings!" Rosalie was more than a little unnerved.

"Most of the time it's best to just give a person a warning, something that the soul understands. Few people heed such admonitions. Most of us tend to wind up learning our lessons the hard way," Timothy said with a sigh as he walked toward the door. "It is time for me to leave you now."

Rosalie nervously glanced around the now dimly lit room, undone by Honey's premonition of her early earthly exit. "So how long will you be gone?"

"Don't worry your pretty head, lass. I'll be back." His words were paternal and caring, like the grandfather she had never had.

"So, how long?" she persisted.

"Long enough for you to have your rest. It is time for the dark night of the soul. Pleasant sleep. Pleasant dreams," and all at once he was gone from sight.

What a strange place, Rosalie thought. People disappearing. People who read your mind. People who tell you Divine Mind is listening. People who travel around in rowboats in black suits and her in a neighborhood without locks. Strange, yet nice, she thought.

Gradually, Rosalie began to unwind while taking in the regal splendor of her new bedroom in her new house beside a beautiful lake.

It was dark outside now. The lamps beside the bed were on. Just as with the television, there were no wires or switches. What a fabulous place, she thought, as she slipped into the pretty yellow nightgown, for she suddenly felt sleepy, dreamy—a simple contentment, as she turned back the bedspread to find white satin sheets trimmed in lace.

"Oh, my God!" she whispered aloud, as she eagerly slipped between the sheets and became instantly enchanted by the silken sensations against her unfleshly flesh. There was no doubt about it. For Rosalie, this was heaven.

The golden mist once more surrounded her, and the music of the spheres serenaded her as a tender, infinite love pervaded her very being to the core. Rosalie now drifted off into a deep, peaceful, dreamless sleep—the dark night of the soul. ✻

Chapter Five

The white sun rose high in the heavens. Another day was dawning. Birds sang in the treetops as Rosalie began to stir from her long night's sleep. Before opening her eyes she tried to remember everything that had taken place. Would Timothy be there? Had it all been some kind of incredible dream? Would she really find herself in a brass canopy bed in a white colonial house across from a magnificent lake somewhere in eternity? Had she really crossed over into another dimension? Rosalie slightly moved one foot. No question, percale sheets from Penney's bargain basement never felt like that. They were satin all right. She quickly opened her eyes.

The room was just as she remembered—fit for the Queen of Sheba or Marie Antoinette. Sunlight streamed in through the French windows and doors. There were fresh daisies in a vase near the door. Yellow daisies. She rubbed the sleep from her eyes while joyfully slithering around on her white satin sheets in a seductive, girlish stretch. Such luxury. Such pleasure she felt as she propped herself up on one elbow to take in the beauty of the room—her dream come true.

She kicked back the covers, wiggling her toes, wondering whether Jean Harlow had the same setup? Probably not, she thought. Harlow's taste would be much more Hollywood. Rosalie thought her own taste was more like *Madame*

Bovary. Aunt Harriet claimed it was a dirty book, but then, Aunt Harriet thought fairy tales were obscene.

Too bad some handsome prince hadn't come to awaken her on this particular morning, Rosalie mused. After all, it was the perfect setting.

That was the moment she realized that she didn't have morning mouth. Strange, she thought, after waking up with morning mouth for the better part of twenty-nine years. She felt no special need to bathe either, yet yearned to try out her sunken Jacuzzi for the pure joy of it. *Cleanliness is next to godliness,* Mama always told her. So she got out of bed and was headed for the bathroom when she heard the sound of a lawnmower in the backyard.

Through seemingly no will of her own she went to the open French doors and out onto the balcony with its abundance of potted and hanging plants. Fuchsias. Creeping Charlies. Giant ferns. Fichus. Wandering Jew. Subtle, she thought, Divine Mind has a sense of humor.

For some reason she wasn't talking to herself. She was in a quiet place. She felt rested and refreshed as she leaned forward on the railing and took in a deep breath of air. The sun was high in the heavens. The temperature was just right. It felt like spring in California, much warmer than New York— not as nippy.

Looking over the landscape, she had to admit it wasn't quite Tara. But then, she had never felt that much sympathy for Scarlett O'Hara. Any woman dumb enough to treat Rhett Butler like that deserved to be scorned. To Rosalie's way of thinking, Scarlett had been a selfish, stupid woman.

Two white doves landed on the railing next to her. Rosalie was enchanted. The air was filled with the songs of birds. Two yellow, orange, and white butterflies appeared in front of her before fluttering on down into the backyard. That was when she saw *him.* At first she couldn't believe her eyes. There *he* was, standing right in the middle of the lawn with a big smile on his face.

"Good morning!" he called out, waving.

He was about six feet tall, and was not wearing a shirt. His skin was golden. He had great shoulders. What a chest! His black hair was thick and curly, glistening in the morning light. He was so handsome. So male. So magnificent. All she could think of saying was, "You must be the prince."

He laughed and replied, "Afraid not. I'm just Manuel." His smile displayed a mouth filled with fabulous white teeth—all straight. "Did I wake you up with the lawn-mower?"

He is so beautiful, she thought to herself. She was trans-fixed. This had to be heaven. David didn't have shoulders like that. Not that they were so bad—just underdeveloped. She stared, shaking her head in answer to his question. David was skinny. This guy wasn't skinny. He had a great body!

"If it's all right with you I'll just go ahead with the gar-dening?" He seemed to be waiting for her permission.

"Sure," she finally managed. "Be my guest."

Manuel nodded, and sauntered back over to the lawnmower. He was barefooted and appeared to be wear-ing only faded blue jeans.

For the moment she just stood there, gaping. Then she ran back into the bedroom. To hell with the Jacuzzi. What if he finished and left before she got dressed? It was only right she should meet the guy who mowed her lawn.

"If only I'd known it would be like this, it would have been okay to die sooner," she said to herself in the mirror. "Look what I've been missing!"

He was obviously Latino. Mama wouldn't approve, of course, but what Mama didn't know couldn't possibly hurt her. Clark Gable may not have been Jewish either. And David, well—he was probably the merry widower by now. Besides, she had heard stories about vacuum cleaner salesmen that could curl your hair.

After all, David hadn't been a virgin when he married her. But then, neither had Rosalie. First, there had been Harlan

Meitzloff, who worked at the post office. Sidney Sylvestan was next. Then David. David was a big improvement, especially after Harlan Meitzloff. Harlan hadn't known the first thing about making love to a woman. He didn't even know how to kiss. And the only other guy she had seen up close with a body like Manuel's was Solomon, and that would have been incest because they were first cousins.

She was in such a hurry she nearly put a pink and white gingham sundress on backwards. She slipped into white sandals, then combed her hair with her fingers. It was something she enjoyed doing with it short. Then she took a really deep breath before running down the stairs and out into the backyard.

There he was, standing in the sunlight with shears in his hands, pruning the roses. He was totally absorbed in his work. What a profile! He had a straight patrician nose that was nothing like David's, more like Paul Newman's. His sculpted ears were flat against his head like ears were supposed to be. And his jaw was so strong and determined. Nobody could push this guy around. His hands were so strong and so masculine—he was pruning roses without even wearing gloves. He didn't seem to be the least bit intimidated by the thorns. What a man! Rosalie watched for a long moment before she could think of something to say.

"So...you're the gardener!" She suddenly felt shy and just knew that she must have a silly smile on her face. She could just feel it.

"You could say that," he replied, thoughtfully. "It's something I really enjoy doing."

"Are you...a gardening angel?" she asked, the silly smile still there.

He threw back his head and laughed. "Not quite. But that's a good one. Very clever! I wonder why nobody else has thought of that one before?"

"It just popped right into my head," she said, grinning. "Dumb, huh? I mean, really dumb!"

❋

"Not dumb. Clever. Really clever."

"I don't know that much about roses." She felt so shy. "I've always pruned at them. I don't really know what I'm doing. I've always meant to read a book about it or something, so I could really learn how to do it right."

"No need." His soft smile with all those flashing white teeth nearly took her breath away. "I'll be glad to show you," he said, suddenly feeling shy. "There's nothing to it, really. You just have to know a few simple facts, and that's all there is to it."

As he carefully snipped here and there amongst the thorny rose branches, Rosalie was entranced. He seemed so sure of himself, so confident.

"If you're not an angel or a prince, what are you?" she asked.

He thought for a moment, then said, "I'm a dead Puerto Rican working my way through the school of higher learning." He tried to keep a straight face but couldn't. He laughed at himself.

"You're putting me on!" She laughed too.

"It's the truth! I swear it." He held up his right hand in an oath.

It all seemed so ridiculous that they both laughed. He had tickled her funny bone, as Papa would say.

"Oh, my God!" Rosalie said, holding her sides. "I had no idea that dying would be so funny."

"Laughter is good for the soul," he said in an attempt to be serious, then he winked.

For an instant she could swear she saw silver stars twinkle in each of his eyes.

"I hear you're awful at fixing TV antennas. Lucky for you we don't have them around here," he went on saying.

"Thank God for that," she was forced to agree.

"Amen. You wouldn't want to go that way again."

"You can die more than once?" was Rosalie's surprised response.

"Well, there are rumors..." he replied, then continued offhandedly, "Don't mind me. Welcome to Lakeside. I know you're going to love it here. It's a great neighborhood."

"How long have you been here?" she asked, beginning to feel more at ease.

"Me? I've been around a while. Actually, I've lost track of time." He got a faraway look in his eyes. "All I remember is, the year right before I died, the Brooklyn Dodgers won the World Series."

"I don't know much about baseball," she admitted. "And I hate to be the one to have to tell you, but the Dodgers don't play in Brooklyn anymore. Now they're based in L.A."

"You see what happens when you go and die? People go crazy. Really crazy. I guess it's just my karma."

"Your what?" She frowned.

"You'll learn about that when you get around to taking classes." Manuel took a clipping from a pink rosebush and handed her a partially opened bloom. "I hear you'll be taking yours on educational TV. Not bad."

Rosalie shyly accepted the flower, inhaling its spicy fragrance. "You mean they have educational television here?"

"They have everything here. They are really ahead of the times, if you know what I mean." He chuckled at his own joke.

"I should hope so. I mean, heaven knows."

"It sure does. They're very tricky here though. Talk about one-upsmanship—you ain't seen nothing yet."

He was so friendly, so open. Not at all macho or arrogant like so many of the really good-looking men she had met. It looked like guys here were different. Even so, she couldn't seem to stop herself from saying what was on her mind.

"What I'm about to ask may sound like a pretty silly request," she hesitated, but just had to ask him, "but would it bother you a whole lot if I...touched you?"

"Heck no! Be my guest."

His reply was so straightforward and innocent, she guessed he didn't have a lecherous bone in his entire heavenly body. He simply held out his hand with an understanding look on his face.

Initially, she hesitated, putting an uncertain finger to her lips. Then she took a deep breath, staring him straight in the eye, and she reached out, stopping just short of his extended hand with its outstretched fingers. A special magnetism was drawing her, a distinct pull she could feel—like touching without touching. It was like chemistry, and yet, it was like nothing she had ever experienced before. Strange, she thought. She wanted to touch him but something was holding her back. She guessed she didn't want him to turn out to be an illusion.

"Go ahead, I know how you feel. I've been there," his voice was gentle, reassuring. His dark brown eyes looked deeply into hers. There was a real connection. "There's nothing to be afraid of. Go on, take my hand."

Rosalie let out a sigh and touched his hand. He wasn't an illusion. He was real. Tangible. His hand was warm, vibrant, strong—the hand of a man.

"Are you sure you're dead?" she asked, quite serious.

"As dead as you are," he replied. "Dead isn't. Life is. Change is. But there is no death. There is only living in many different dimensions. We happen to be in one of them."

"So how did you die?" she asked. His eyes were so intense she was forced to look away. "Would you mind talking about it? I mean, was it a street fight, switchblades?"

"No *West Side Story* for me, little lady. Nothing nearly so romantic." He paused, taking a dramatic pose before saying, "I was creamed by a cab on 57th in Manhattan, right in the middle of the intersection, with the signal blinking, *Don't Walk!* My folks couldn't even collect money from the stupid cab company because I was jaywalking. How bad is that?"

"I don't know what's dumber—that or falling off a roof after being bombed by a stupid blackbird," Rosalie replied, all smiles.

They both laughed.

"I mean, breaking your neck is hardly romantic. Why couldn't I have gotten consumption and died in style like Camille?"

"Right," Manuel agreed. "Death-bed drama."

"How old are you, anyway?" Rosalie asked point-blank.

"God knows. Age isn't either. That's another grand illusion," he replied, snipping another rosebud from a bush, a white one, which he handed to her.

"When I departed from the great state of New York in the U.S. of A., I was pushing thirty-two and holding. Naturally that was before I got splattered all over 57th and Fifth Avenue. That undertaker had one hell of a job on his hands—that cab was moving right along. You see, there were two cars involved, so you could truly say that I was a broken man."

"Spare me the gory details, please," she responded with a shudder.

"Sorry. I didn't mean to offend you. But it doesn't matter now anyway. It's all over and done with." He looked deeply into her eyes as he said, "And here I am in paradise talking to a pretty girl in a pink gingham dress and her name is Rosalie. I love your name. I had a sister named Rosa."

"I was named after my great-grandmother on my father's side," she replied, suddenly feeling shy again. "Do you really think that I'm pretty? I've never actually thought of myself as being very pretty."

"I think you're beautiful! Festival of roses, that's what your name means. Roses are my favorite flowers. Your soul possesses the beauty of a rose."

"Oh, you mean you think I have a beautiful soul." The expression on her face was one of disappointment.

"No. That's not what I mean," he protested, holding up both hands. "Not that I mean to say that your soul isn't beautiful. It is. It's just that you're beautiful...all over," he quickly added, glancing at the ground in mild embarrassment; then he looked into her eyes with a sheepish grin as he commented, "Here we all have heavenly bodies."

Rosalie studied him. His eyes were soft, glowing. His skin looked smooth and it was so golden. Funny this should happen, she thought. She had never been attracted to Puerto Ricans when she lived in New York. But then, Mama would have had a fit if she had even thought of dating an ordinary Gentile, let alone a golden one.

"Did you have a wife?" she asked him.

"No wife, no kids. Three brothers, two sisters, a mother, a father, one dog, three cats, and a parakeet," he replied. "And four goldfish. The goldfish actually belonged to my kid sister, Theresa, but I fed them most of the time, so I always considered them part mine. After all, I was the one who named them."

"So what did you name them?" she asked. She was beginning to feel that telltale tingly sensation in the pit of her stomach.

"Moby Dick, Jonah, Sassafras, and White Death," he said with a straight face.

"White Death? You named a goldfish White Death?"

"He was white, and he was the runt of the litter. I thought maybe if I named him after a shark that it would help him keep the other guys in line. Besides, he nearly died three times." His thoughts drifted, remembering his past with mixed emotions. "Theresa never did like the names."

"What sort of work did you do?"

"What is this, the third degree?" he inquired without sounding defensive.

"I've always thought the best way to get to know someone is by asking questions. Sorry."

"Don't be sorry. Just don't expect me to answer all of them. I've never liked playing twenty questions."

"Were you a gardener?" Something made her ask.

"No, my dear," he replied, shaking his head with an amused smile on his face. "But my father was a gardener on

Long Island, and he took care of some pretty jazzy lawns. When I was a kid I used to tag along with him whenever he would let me. I worked along beside him. My father taught me everything I know about Mother Nature. Gardening has always made me feel free, closer to God. It was a wonderful time, and a chance to be alone with my father, who was truly a great man. He was kind but tough, hard-working but gentle. He loved the earth and helping plants to grow. Maybe I should have been a gardener." He looked into her searching eyes, but she didn't say anything. She just waited.

"I was an architectural draftsman," he finally told her. "It was my big dream to become an architect, to leave my own special mark on the sands of time, to design spectacular structures that would outlast the Pyramids of Giza. The closest I ever got was helping to design an electrical system for a new city waterworks in Queens. Not a very great contribution, I'll admit, but I did manage to help save the city forty thousand bucks with the system's design."

"Hey, that's terrific!" Rosalie replied. After all, to her it sounded a lot more glamorous than selling vacuum cleaners in the San Fernando Valley.

David's eyes were brown, too, but they usually looked muddy. Manuel's eyes reminded her of chocolate, and Rosalie had a weakness for chocolate.

Rosalie was younger and prettier than most of the other new arrivals Manuel had met. Most of the other women had been over fifty. Mama would have been upset if Manuel found a Jewish girl more than just attractive. But then, Mama would probably have been upset if he had found any girl attractive. It would have meant another mouth to feed, or losing his income entirely. Mama could be possessive of her children, especially her Manuel.

Children represented the earning power that Mama hoped would support her better one day than Papa ever had. Poor Mama. She had lost a breadwinner. At least she had received the ten thousand dollars from the life insurance. It was the most money she had ever seen at one time in her life. For a moment, Mama felt rich. But the money had never filled the empty place left in her heart.

"I see that the two of you have become acquainted," Father Timothy said, appearing from out of nowhere. It was plain to see that Manuel and Rosalie were captivated with one another.

Rosalie finally took her eyes off Manuel. "I was beginning to wonder just what had happened to you," her voice was soft as she spoke. "I thought maybe you'd forsaken me."

"Now, now," he replied, good-naturedly. "I could hardly do that, now could I?" He noted the changes in her energy field with heartfelt approval. "Did you have a nice rest, lass?"

"Oh, yes. I've never slept so peacefully. At least not that I can remember."

Timothy and Manuel exchanged knowing smiles.

Manuel sensed it was lesson time for Rosalie, so he turned to her to say, "I'm afraid it's time for me to go."

All at once she became apprehensive. He, too, hesitated. Being near her, sensing her vibrations had begun to stir something deep and strong within him, something he did not yet fully understand. She, too, could sense a hidden, special meaning in their meeting.

"I'll see you again, won't I?" she felt the need to ask.

"Absolutely. Manuel Sierra has promised to teach you how to prune roses, and he is a man of his word." This was something he had learned from his father, too. He gallantly bowed to her.

"Don't feel like you have to teach me, that is, unless you want to," she was giving him a way out. It felt like butterflies were fluttering in her stomach.

"I want to," he said, looking right into her eyes.

His smile was so wonderful, she thought she would melt on the spot.

Then he continued, "All promises should be so light a task and for such a fair lady."

"Are you sure you weren't a poet?" Rosalie chided.

"Only on Tuesday and Thursday evenings when I took creative writing classes at City College," he replied.

The very same nights that David took writing classes. She hesitated before saying, "My husband, David, took writing classes, too. He was writing a book when he could find the time. I don't know how good it was. I liked it. He seemed to be working at it very hard."

"Don't we all?" Manuel replied, his expression now serious. In a sudden change of mood, he grabbed her hand, bowed and kissed it. "Parting is such sweet sorrow, and all that jazz. Adios, beautiful lady. Vaya con Dios."

"You, too," she said, holding her breath, and she watched him walk toward the side of the house, where he vanished in a golden mist.

Another miracle, she thought, turning to Timothy, misty-eyed, to say, "Being dead is terrific. Mama mia! How many more guys like that do you have around here?"

"I'm pleased that you like Manuel. I'm rather partial to him myself."

"Partial's a nice word," she replied, grinning.

She gazed at her hand where he had kissed it, lightly touching it with her fingertips. No one had ever done anything like that before. She lifted the pink and white rosebuds to her nose to inhale their sweet fragrance—blossoms he had picked especially for her.

Timothy was admiring the garden. "He does such a beautiful job with the roses, don't you think?"

"Absolutely," Rosalie agreed, a warm glow in her heart. "Which means that he's going to do a terrific job with me. You see, I'm a festival of roses." 🌸

Chapter Six

"Too bad Honey isn't here." Rosalie was brewing tea. "She could read our tea leaves. Ides of March and raven's wings! How was I supposed to know what that meant? She was talking in riddles."

"She probably didn't know herself," Timothy informed her. "Many intuitive people receive images and feelings they don't always completely understand until after the event occurs. When it involves tragedy it can be very upsetting for them."

"Upsetting for them! How do you think it makes me feel?" She was pouring Timothy a cup of tea. "Honey or sugar?"

"Neither, thank you. I'll take mine straight."

Rosalie poured honey into her tea and stirred with vigor. Then she sat down at the table across from Timothy. She was in a pensive mood, and Timothy was quiet. It was a bright, sunny kitchen, in accordance with her imaginary taste. So they sat there together, drinking tea and gazing out the window. Sailboats glided on the lake. Everything was so idyllic.

Rosalie surmised that it wasn't a bad place to spend eternity, but on the other hand, the house was awfully big and quiet and more or less empty with just her there.

"I noticed some cats when we first got here—down the street on someone's lawn. I guess that means it's all right to have pets around here."

Timothy took a sip of tea and watched her closely. "Jasmine?" he inquired.

"Yeah. Do you like jasmine?"

"It happens to be one of my favorites. I'm also very fond of strawberry tea."

"I've never had strawberry tea. Can we get some?"

"Naturally," he assured her. Timothy was trying to tune in on her thoughtforms. "Did you have a pet on earth?"

"David wouldn't let me. He said we couldn't afford a dog. He wanted me to go back to work at the supermarket so we could save enough money to buy our own home. He said if I went to work, a dog would have to be left alone, and that would be lousy for the dog. And besides that, David was afraid a dog might tear things up—dig up the yard, or chew up David's slippers, which he doesn't have and never would wear if he did, because David even hates shoes. Honey said it's because he's a Pisces, and Pisces rules the feet, but I don't believe in that astrology crap, do you?"

Timothy was amazed with her train of thought, finally asking, "Do I what?"

"Believe in astrology, horoscopes, that sort of thing?" She finished her tea and took a cookie out of a large jar on the table.

"I suppose that I do," Timothy cautiously stated.

"Oh, yeah? Well, I thought religious people considered astrology the work of the devil. My Aunt Harriet always said that Moses warned the children of Israel against soothsayers. She claimed it says so in the Torah. I mean, they not only burned witches in Salem—they stoned them in Sinai to boot. That's why Aunt Harriet didn't like Honey. You see, Honey was not only a Gentile. She was a fortune-telling Gentile. That did it for Aunt Harriet. She said Honey was meshuga. That's Yiddish for crazy." Rosalie dutifully rinsed her cup, an old habit.

"Your Aunt Harriet sounds like a rather opinionated woman," Timothy noted without malice.

"You can say that again. And so Jewish she makes Moses look Gentile. And you know what else she is?"

Timothy simply shook his head, waiting to be informed.

"She's a frustrated Jewish mother without any kids. That's what she is. An old maid. Poor Aunt Harriet. Poor kids, if she had ever had any. God knew what he was doing when he allowed that woman to keep her virginity. She never got laid in her life. Papa always said that was Aunt Harriet's problem. All she needed was a good screw. It would have changed her entire life."

Timothy stared straight ahead, blushing, praying that he would soon adjust to Rosalie's energy field.

"Do you mean to tell me that the stars and the planets really have something to do with our lives?" She took another cookie out of the jar. "Would you like one?"

"No, thank you."

Eating in that dimension was unnecessary, a simple matter of choice. Timothy was still trying to realign his energy field. Sexual topics had never been his strong point. He was still thinking about Aunt Harriet. Nonetheless, he took a deep breath and began speaking, "Patterns formed by planetary energy interaction set up vibratory frequencies that affect the core of each soul as it enters the earth's atmosphere at the time of birth. These energy patterns in turn create vortexes that help determine the destiny to which the soul will be drawn. Each soul, however, is endowed with the free will of the Creator, and is only directionally impelled, and not necessarily compelled, to act out the preordained patterns." He sounded like he was reading from a textbook.

"Hey! Wait a minute!" Rosalie protested with upraised hands. "Could you repeat that again in plain English? Vortexes, frequencies, impel, compel. What the hell does it all mean? I ask you a simple question, and you come back sounding like Albert Einstein."

"Actually," he replied, looking sheepish, "I'm just learning about such things myself. The information I just gave you is from my homework. I suppose a simpler explanation would be that our horoscope, while we're on earth, is a blueprint or map for our soul. The blueprint indicates character, talents, and skills capable of being developed during our lifetime, and yet, each soul has the freedom to build from that blueprint in any number of ways to reach the same or a similar destination."

"You learned all that stuff in school here? It isn't enough you have to go to school on earth?" Heaven was full of surprises. That was when she remembered that Manuel had said something about educational television.

"Learning is an eternal process, lass. Are you trying to tell me you already know everything there is to know?"

"Hell, no! I barely made it through high school with a C average. I was lucky to graduate from the platform, so I became a grocery checker. Big deal! I can add, subtract, and multiply, and I didn't even have to do that because the cash register does it for you. The only thing I was really good at was math. But Mama always said never let a guy know you're good at math or you'll end up an old maid. So I kept my mouth shut and still didn't land a husband until I was twenty-five. So what good did it do me, I ask you?"

Timothy did not have an answer.

"Maybe if I had let a guy know that I could add two and two sooner, he would have kept me around to balance his checkbook. That's what finally happened. David was lousy at math. Imagine, a vacuum cleaner salesman who can't add or subtract—that's a definite handicap."

"It seems that it would be." Rosalie's thought processes were definitely something of a challenge.

"Do you suppose I could have a dog?"

The question seemed to come from out of nowhere. It took Timothy a minute to get his bearings. "Did you ever have a dog on earth?"

"Well, not exactly," Rosalie hedged. "Except when I lived in Brooklyn when I was a kid, there was this shaggy little black mutt that used to follow me around. He wasn't really mine. He sort of belonged to the neighborhood. But I used to pretend that he was mine, because one time he nearly took a chunk out of this kid who lived on the next block when he tried to push me around and steal my roller skates. That's why I named him Irving. Irving was the name of my favorite uncle who lived in New Jersey. Uncle Irving always protected me whenever anybody tried to push me around." She paused for a moment, a faraway look in her eyes. "I never knew whether Uncle Irving was really pleased when I told him I'd named the dog after him, but he should have been. Irving was a very brave dog. He was a genuine hero. Irving saved Herbie's life."

"And who was Herbie?" Timothy inquired.

"My second cousin on my mother's side; he lived in the Bronx. Do you want to hear the story?"

How could he refuse? Timothy patiently prepared to listen.

"Well, it was like this," she began, getting into her dramatic mode. "One day Herbie was antagonizing this German shepherd with a big stick, which naturally, he shouldn't have been doing—and the dog went for him." She grabbed her throat with both hands.

"Was I scared! I held my breath. I didn't know what to do. Then it happened. Irving came galloping to the rescue. I guess dogs don't really gallop, but Irving sure looked like he was galloping. Anyway, he tore into that German shepherd like he was a Doberman or something. That little black mutt was ferocious! It was awesome. And Irving didn't weigh more than thirty pounds soaking wet, and the shepherd was a monster—easily a hundred and forty pounds! But do you think that could stop Irving? Not my Irving! He was a tiger. Inside, he was the biggest goddamn dog in the whole world!" She stopped for a moment as tears filled her eyes. "So the

German shepherd killed Irving instead of my cousin Herbie." Tears now rolled down both cheeks.

"The pound took the shepherd away in a muzzle. He'd terrorized the whole neighborhood for a long time. There wasn't any place to bury Irving, so the sanitation department came and got him. It was awful. I cried for a week. Not that I wished it'd been Herbie. God forbid! He wasn't that big a brat. It was just that Irving was such a great dog." A faraway look formed in her eyes. "And something I can tell you for sure—Herbie never antagonized another dog in his life. He knew it could have been him instead of Irving. I really thought Herbie was done for when it all started. He still has a scar on his throat to this day. It took thirty-two stitches to put his throat back together again." She shivered, remembering the awful scene.

"Irving was as terrific as dogs come," she said. "He was a genuine dog hero." Rosalie brushed the tears from her cheeks. "I sure did love that crazy little black mutt."

A strange smile formed on Timothy's lips as the bark of a dog was heard in the backyard. Rosalie was still caught up in reverie, remembering Irving, his heroic actions in saving a boy he considered his friend. "When animals die, do they come here, too?" she asked.

Again, the bark of a dog could be heard.

Father Timothy then walked over to the Dutch door and looked out into the backyard. "A shaggy, black mutt, you say? About thirty pounds?"

Again, the dog barked—this time from directly outside the kitchen door.

Rosalie's eyes widened in disbelief. The dog was now barking and barking, insisting that someone respond to his needs. Rosalie shivered and broke out in large goose bumps, then got up and ran to the door. It was Irving. Irving was barking and barking and jumping for joy.

Out in the yard Rosalie fell to her knees, gathering the squirming black mutt into her arms. Tears of joy filled her eyes, streaming down her cheeks.

✻

"Oh, Irving! Irving! You're here!" she wept, hugging the dog tightly, yet he managed to squirm free, licking her face to express his own joy.

It was difficult to tell which one was more excited— Rosalie or Irving. When the dog finally managed to get all four feet on the ground, Rosalie gently held his face in her hands as his entire body wagged along with his tail.

"Dear, adorable Irving," she managed between tears. "I thought I'd never see you again. Never! But here you are. And here I am." She hugged him again, still sobbing.

Timothy handed her a handkerchief, tears in his eyes.

"Oh, Timothy, thank you, thank you so much. How can I ever thank you enough?" She blew her nose with one hand while continuing to pet Irving with the other.

"Don't thank me," Timothy replied, overwhelmed with emotion. "Thank God." Tears rolled down his cheeks.

Rosalie tried hard to regain self-control but she couldn't stop crying. Irving was jumping up and down and all around—his tail still wagging. Then he ran out into the yard, playfully barking. Irving didn't want his mistress to cry.

"Is it really him?" she asked, wiping away the years. "Tell me it's really him."

"Oh, yes," Timothy assured her. "He's been waiting for you for quite some time."

"You mean, all this time nobody wanted him?" Rosalie was appalled.

"Oh, come now, everyone wanted him. He's had lots of company. After all, dog heroes are a favorite here, too. You should hear some of the stories."

Rosalie was beginning to calm down, trying to stop crying; but now Timothy was beginning to sniffle.

"I have an Irish setter. Her name is Penny—short for Penelope. I'll bring her along sometime. She and Irving should be great friends."

Rosalie threw her arms around Timothy. "You dear, sweet man," she cried, "I only hope that everyone who dies and comes here meets someone just like you." She kissed his cheek. "You have no idea just how special you are!"

"You're pretty special yourself, lass," he replied, hugging her back. "Pretty special yourself," he said again, wiping the tears from his eyes.

Irving was barking, demanding attention—the way only dogs know how to do. So Rosalie turned, feeling much like a child again, and ran into the backyard to play with her dog. When she finally turned to look for Timothy, he was nowhere in sight.

For the moment it didn't matter. She had Irving, and they had lots of catching up to do. How nice, she thought, that dogs do keep on living, too. How kind of God to allow it. ✿

Chapter Seven

Timothy was traveling at the speed of thought—something he really enjoyed doing since he had gotten the knack of it. Just close his eyes, focus his mind's eye on the place he wanted to be, and bingo! There he was. He had never been able to do that on earth. But then, he hadn't been on earth for a hundred years.

During Timothy's time there was a Civil War in the New World—America. A man named Abraham Lincoln was being talked about in the British Isles. President Lincoln had crossed over since, of course. Timothy had seen him once, but they had never really met. He had never been all that interested in politics, though lately there had been talk that the soul of Lincoln had returned to further aid a nation less divided but still in need of help—particularly when it came to getting people to accept one another regardless of race, color, or creed.

Word was out that the Hierarchy was counting on America. The coin of the realm held the motto *In God We Trust*. Souls seeking religious freedom had originally migrated to America—freedom from persecution and hatred. Timothy hoped the Irish were doing their part to aid in America's evolution.

Timothy O'Toole had been a parish priest in County Cork, Ireland, a humble priest with a modest congregation of Catholics. During his time the Church of England had been amassing converts at a rapid rate. Protestantism had definitely caught on. So with the Irish migrations to America and the awful potato blight, there were not that many parishioners left. Father Timothy's flock dwindled to a mere twenty souls. Only some bothered to take communion, let alone honor the confessional. But then, that was long ago. Since Timothy had crossed over, plenty of souls had been in need of his attention.

The work was different here—broader in scope. Souls were simply souls, regardless of race, color, religion, or station. All were evolving. All were in need of nurturing and love. Timothy enjoyed his assignments for the most part, and he was growing very fond of Rosalie. Aspects of her character bothered him a bit, though—which was why he decided to pay a visit to Marcella.

Marcella's marble temple always held Timothy in such awe. It was Grecian in design with a dozen alabaster pillars all around. Great fountains overflowed with pure, crystalline water. Commanding marble statues sculpted by masters of the trade adorned the hall. Marcella had been a vestal virgin in Rome during a favorite lifetime. Earlier, in Greece, she had served as an oracle for the Sun god at the Temple of Apollo at Delphi. Marcella was no slouch. An Initiate of the illustrious Eleusinian mysteries, there was talk that she had also been one of the queens of ancient Egypt. Her unusual beauty was a classical mixture of the Roman and the Greek, and suited her present self-image.

A woman of great mystery, Marcella rarely discussed her prior achievements. It was said that somewhere on earth her image was etched in stone, enduring the tests of time. Her Greek and Roman embodiments provided her happiest and most lasting memories, so now she surrounded herself with the beauty she had known then.

To each his own, Timothy thought to himself, for he never felt totally comfortable in Marcella's temple. It was much too grand for him. He preferred his cottage on the heath where the heather bloomed continuously—its sweet fragrance wafting upon a steady though gentle breeze.

The temple stood on an island atop sheer rock cliffs, where the mighty ocean sent majestic waves crashing to their destiny. Marcella loved the aura of privacy—solitude combined with the eternal murmur of the ever-restless sea. All who sought her special wisdom were free to come and go as the Spirit moved them. Banquets were often held there—festivals to celebrate the equinoxes. Marcella was especially fond of welcoming the Summer Solstice in remembrance of Apollo's ancient reign. Her earthly heritage remained dear to her heart, adding a special flavor to her soul's identity.

"Welcome, Timothy," she called out in a lyrical voice the moment his presence was sensed. Marcella had a gift for instantly identifying each vibration in her charge. She was wearing a long, flowing, diaphanous white gown gathered to a point of decency, a golden belt of a serpent swallowing its own tail—the symbol of eternity—encircling her waist. An ivory rose brooch secured a royal blue cape about her shoulders. In the sunlight, the silver thread woven into the metallic fabric reflected a multitude of sparkling points of light. Her long, golden hair was piled upon her head, a starburst sapphire securing it in place. Her luminous blue eyes gracefully accented by delicate arched eyebrows were penetrating yet loving.

The compassionate magnetism that was unmistakably Marcella always made Timothy feel at a temporary loss for words. She was utter femininity: womanhood crowned and enthroned. Every time he saw her it was difficult for him to remember why he had chosen celibacy during his last life. He knew it would be different next time. It had to be after experiencing the presence of Marcella, even though he surmised Marcella would never return to earth. Having evolved to a position of considerable responsibility in the Hierarchy of Light, Marcella was needed at a higher level on the evolutionary spiral.

Marcella was smiling. Naturally, she had read Timothy's thoughts. She was the most evolved Being he had yet been privileged to meet, and there was talk she had a counterpart, a true soulmate—Matthias. Timothy hoped to meet him one day.

"Top o' the morning, Mother Superior," he finally managed, beaming from head to toe. He always felt like such a helpless child in her presence, though he appeared an old man and she a woman in her prime.

Her eyes sparkled. He delighted her so. Such a dear soul, Timothy. He was trying so hard and had come such a long way. She gave him a warm hug and a brief kiss on his blushing cheek. "I love you, Timothy," she said, and appeared to float by him with her feet off the ground. "You are a dear, sweet, wonderful soul."

Her movements were as feminine as a finely trained dancer, for she was one who always danced at the festival of the Summer Solstice. Light was always cause for great joy, so Marcella celebrated and danced often. She said she was dancing the Dance of Life.

"When will you cease to hold me in such awe, dear Timothy?" she scolded, then laughed. Her laughter was like a song. "I am simply Marcella, a soul much like yourself."

"Hardly like me," Timothy objected, lowering his eyes in embarrassment, as he sputtered, "I have a masculine vehicle, and besides that, I'm short, stout, and old."

"But that is the way you choose to be," she informed him with a slight tone of chastisement. "You can be anything you want to be, appear any way you choose to appear. I choose to be as I am because I have merged with the sphere of beauty at the Center. And besides that, I'm vain." She threw back her head in a peal of girlish laughter.

"I can hardly think of the likes of you as being vain, my dear, sweet, beautiful lady," Timothy protested. "Why, you're a bit of heaven, you are." His eyes twinkled. "The purest, finest, most decent lass I've ever had the privilege to gaze upon in all eternity."

"You've kissed the Blarney stone, Timothy O'Toole," she playfully proclaimed, again throwing her head back in a melodious ring of laughter. "Faith and begorra, dear man," she affected an Irish brogue, "there was plenty a fair lass in Ireland during your time, dimpled darlin's running through the heather. But you were such a bookish lad and so wrapped up in dedicating your life to the Virgin Mary that you found no time for the pursuit of other virgins."

When Timothy blushed in reply, Marcella could not suppress a giggle. "Dear, sweet Timothy, you must go back one day. There is so much more for you to learn from life on earth, for woman must not only be worshiped from afar—though that is a fine and noble ideal, I grant you—but you must learn firsthand that woman is a part of you, and you a part of woman."

Once again she affected a lilting Irish brogue, "It just takes a wee bit of time to get the two halves properly joined, as well as infinite patience. You'll see one day, dear Timothy. And I'm sure that you'll get the hang of it."

"I'm not quite ready to return yet, thank you just the same," he protested, flustered by the mere suggestion. "I'm on assignment, you know." He straightened his frock and squared his shoulders to appear more dignified.

"Yes, Timothy, I know." She playfully cleared her throat, then smiled her mystical smile as she glided toward the edge of the temple to face the open sea. "Rosalie is delightful, is she not?"

"A dear, sweet lass, Marcella," he started out, "though I do wish you could do something about her language. She takes the Lord's name in vain so frequently, saying things like *I'll be damned*, that I fear one day she will be."

Marcella laughed. Wisps of her blonde hair danced in the ocean breeze as she turned to face him, a serious expression forming on her face. "My dear Timothy, after all you have learned here, how can you even allow such thoughts to enter your mind? Rosalie Rosenberg is a jewel compared to many souls that have reached this level. An innocent conditioned by her upbringing and the society in which she lived. Hellfire is in no way intended for the likes of Rosalie. During her twenty-nine year sojourn on earth, she never once entertained the thought of going to hell, and she certainly never conducted herself in any manner that would warrant her receiving such measures.

"Am I to remind you," she continued, "that most of the souls who enter such a state for any period of time are either temporarily deserving, due to grievous acts of inhumanity toward their fellow man or woman, or are simply souls who have consistently feared such conditions throughout their earthly existence. For such souls the state may be created in accordance with their innermost fears, which is sad but true. And even in such dismal cases, as you well know, the deplorable condition does not last. It cannot last and will not last in spite of all the ill-informed souls who insist on misinterpreting revelations that have been transmitted to earth over the ages by those higher up in the Hierarchy." Her expression was playfully perplexed as she asked, "After all you have been taught, Timothy, what do you suggest I do with you?"

"Forgive me," he replied, feeling properly chastised. "I guess I still have a great deal to learn."

"We all have a great deal to learn. It's part of the joy of possessing the Divine Spark. Life is an endless, everlasting adventure, Timothy," her voice was jubilant. Marcella loved life more than anyone Timothy had ever known.

"We all must learn to live more fully, to dance the Dance of Life. And to dance with unconditional and absolute joy and love."

As she passed by the Eternal Flame ablaze in the midst of the temple, she paused near an impressive marble statue of a tall, handsome, regal man with a penetrating gaze—a man in his prime dressed in a toga after the manner of ancient Greece. A laurel wreath etched around his curly hair gave him a truly noble bearing. The breeze from the sea ruffled her majestic cape as her white gown whirled as though in a mist about her. Her skin was translucent. For a brief moment her vibratory frequency became so fine that she nearly disappeared. During fleeting intervals she appeared as a vaporous substance pulsating with life endowed with the feminine principle—a spectral prism of dazzling, flashing light.

"I wish I had your attitude," Timothy finally managed. "You have such a positive way of seeing everything. I must say that I always leave here with my spirit renewed."

Timothy loved Marcella with a love that was deep and pure. Much the same as the love he had felt for the Virgin Mother, for Marcella was a sort of cosmic mother figure for many of the souls at that level.

When she turned to him he knew that she had read his thoughts. An overwhelming wave of love passed between them, love that transcended description due to its purity of essence. It generally took Timothy what seemed like several minutes to recover from one of Marcella's love waves. It was pure ecstasy.

"You are love personified," he finally said.

"I am but a Divine reflector. We love in each other that portion we all share. We can only receive as much as we are able to give. The love that you feel for me contains as much joy as the love I return to you. It is just that I am able to see you in your wholeness while, as yet, you only see me in part."

Marcella made Truth palatable. For a moment Timothy meditated on the blissful joy that filled his entire being. She had once revealed to him that they had been childhood friends in ancient Atlantis, and said they had been together many times in this dimension. Timothy was only just starting to remember his former lifetimes. He had learned that past-life memory was something that had to be earned. Still, Timothy couldn't help but wonder how Marcella had been able to evolve so much faster. Why was she so much further ahead of most souls?

"We are all brothers and sisters in the Light, a unity of the Greater Life. We are all growing and developing, and will continue to help one another to attain ever greater Light, Wisdom, and Love. Yet, of course, there is also the matter of Grace. You will understand that much better one day, Timothy." Her smile was radiant as she sat down on a marble bench, her hair glistening in the light as though bedecked with a multitude of tiny sparkling diamonds.

"Why do you always assign me to agnostics and atheists?" Timothy felt compelled to ask. "I've never been given even one Catholic."

Marcella was delighted. "Dear Timothy, we are all God's children! I cannot give you all the answers, else I would rob you of the joy of discovering the Truth for yourself."

Upon removing her sapphire clasp, Marcella's hair cascaded into silken threads about her shoulders. Her exquisite beauty dazzled him once again.

"You are marvelous for my vanity, sweet Timothy." Her eyes twinkled. "You should visit me more often. One day soon we must make plans for your return."

Timothy wasn't prepared to think about leaving that dimension. The very thought saddened him. There was such freedom on that side of life—no physical discomforts. Though he did understand that he would have to return to earth one day. Such facts were always transmitted from higher spheres, sometimes telepathically. Departures were necessary, beyond the need for discussion, although he personally still enjoyed talking with other souls—it was an old habit.

Thought transference was the purest form of communication, but his frequency still needed greater refinement for total rapport at that level. Marcella's constant awareness of his thoughts and feelings before he could express them still tended to unnerve him, though at times it was comforting, too. Every stage of growth continued to produce profoundly mixed emotions for Timothy.

"I suppose that Rosalie is ready to start reviewing," he said with a sigh.

Reviewing was not one of Timothy's favorite things. It could be interesting, granted—though most mortals seemed to make the same mistakes over and over again. It was like playing a broken record on a faulty gramophone. The majority seemed to need several lifetimes to correct one simple character flaw. That was the astonishing part. Reviewing his own past life had not been a pleasant experience for him. He had made his own fair share of mistakes and misjudgments, though his transition had been merciful—a first-rate heart attack at a ripe old age.

Since his first assignment so long ago, he had been present at the awakening and reviewing of many souls. But Rosalie's transition had certainly been unique in his experience. Never before had Timothy been assigned to a case of a broken neck due to a vertiginous crow. The bird's navigational sense had become completely distorted due to a brain tumor. The crow crossed over the very next day. Nature's evolutionary process was obviously still in need of some refinement. With any luck the crow would incarnate as a healthier creature next time around.

Once more, Marcella was gazing out to sea in a state of cosmic reverie, her consciousness at one with the Universal. When observing her in such a state, Timothy felt reverence mixed with wonder. He had yet to experience Cosmic Consciousness, a state to be reached upon the earth first. Most souls at that level still had yet to ascend many turns on the evolutionary spiral. One day Timothy would attain Marcella's state of awareness; it was a state destined for all evolving souls.

"I suppose we'll follow standard procedure and start with the funeral. Is that the plan for Rosalie?" Timothy ventured, somewhat reluctant to awaken Marcella from her cosmic reverie.

Marcella simply nodded, her misty eyes envisioning a distant grandeur, a compassionate expression on her face.

"I don't care much for funerals," Timothy confessed.

"One day there will be no need for such rituals. Consciousness will evolve to that place. It is not far off as the crow flies."

Timothy winced. Her humor sometimes escaped him.

"Was Rosalie's death an accident?" he was forced to ask.

Marcella remained silent.

Timothy had learned that the transition called death was usually predestined, predetermined by the life or character of each soul. Even so, some deaths were still hard for him to understand. There seemed to be so much for him yet to learn.

"Couldn't we just give her a few more presents first?" he implored, remembering Rosalie's happy reunion with Irving.

"It is time for Rosalie to watch television, Timothy. Godspeed. May you both grow in Wisdom, Love, and Understanding." And with that she was gone in a fragrant mist of dazzling, whirling, brilliant light. All that remained was the eternally burning flame. ✻

Chapter Eight

Rosalie was seated in the recliner in the den, eating popcorn by the handful out of a large bowl in her lap. Popcorn was one of her favorite things. She stared impatiently at the large blank television screen.

A fire blazed in the used brick fireplace. Over the large, soft brown leather sofa she could really sink into was the Van Gogh she had always planned to buy, a print of sunflowers. All around the comfy rustic room were special artifacts she had admired at one time or another: Inca, Aztec, Navajo, and that Nefertiti head she had always wanted. Ancient Egypt held a special fascination for Rosalie. Land of the pyramids—land of the Pharaohs.

Irving was curled up in a ball at her feet, snoozing and dreaming dog dreams. The afternoon had been wonderful for both of them, playing fetch with the ball and running beside the lake. They went swimming in the refreshing water. It was perfect, having a dog of her own. Something she had always longed and hoped for. Something she had never had on earth.

Out in the kitchen Timothy was brewing strawberry tea in a china pot painted with purple and yellow violets. Rosalie had begun to wonder if there were supermarkets here, too, like the ones in North Hollywood. Places where she could go shopping. And yet, to her constant amazement, anything

she thought about or wanted seemed to show up in a cupboard, an apothecary jar, or the refrigerator. All she had to
do was think about it. For Rosalie, this was more than amazing. It was unbelievable. Still, it happened.

The television set in the den was the biggest one in the
house, just like she had always wanted, of course. Now
maybe she could really see the faces of those handsome
hunks that starred on her favorite soaps up close, see the
way they kissed their ladies—which could change from week
to week, of course. Now maybe she could discern their hidden motives a little bit better and understand why they did
some of the astonishing and stupid things they did over and
over again. She had tried in vain to find her favorite programs, or any program for that matter, on all the TVs in the
house. Still, no response. It was frustrating her. Not even a
response from the TV in the wall at the foot of the Jacuzzi.

That afternoon she had christened her new marble tub
by enjoying a luxurious soak in lavender bubbles. And the
bubbles really were lavender, not white. Incredible! So for a
moment she forgot about not being able to watch television.

The television set in the living room was in a fancy
French cabinet. The one on the kitchen counter near the
breadbox was smaller but nice. In the dining room there was
another TV inside a cabinet that matched the breakfront.
None of the sets in the entire house had switches, dials, or
wires—and no remote controls in sight. All of her wishing
and hoping and yearning had yet to turn on one single set.
Strange, she thought, very strange. Her only disappointment
as yet.

"Are you sure there's going to be something on?" she
finally asked, stuffing more popcorn into her mouth.

Timothy walked in carrying a tray with biscuits, tea,
and strawberry preserves, which he placed on the coffee
table. Then he happily sank into the soft leather sofa. Divine
comfort. He rather enjoyed Rosalie's taste.

He had exchanged his clerical garb for the standard dress
of his time, which made him look a bit like an oversized

leprechaun, though he did seem to be losing some weight. Marcella's remarks had sparked serious reevaluation. He was beginning to think of himself more in the way he had been when he was a much younger man.

"Patience, lass," came his reply as he took a sip of tea. "Now that's a cup of tea!"

Rosalie stared hard at the blank screen, sipping from a glass of lemonade that had magically appeared beside her. She had not noticed a single servant anywhere in the house. She did, however, remember Honey saying something about there being *administering angels*. For all she knew, they were busy administering right there in her house.

"Perhaps we should have invited Manuel," she said, half-teasing, wondering when she would see him again.

"Not just yet," Timothy replied, a note of caution in his voice.

"Where does he live, anyway?" she tried to sound casual.

"In the mountains."

"You have mountains here, too?"

"We have every conceivable thing that humanity enjoys, plus a trillion, zillion other things mortals have not yet dreamt of. This is the Source, lass! How many times must I tell you?"

"How come he lives in the mountains?" She offered Timothy popcorn, which he declined with a shake of his head.

"I can't understand why anyone wouldn't like popcorn." She chewed and talked at the same time. After swallowing she reminded him, "You didn't answer my question."

"The mountains give Manuel a sense of peace and joy."

"Oh, yeah? Are they far away?" She paused. "Dimensionally speaking?" She grinned.

"No," he replied, beginning to find her quite charming.

"What does he do up there? Prune a lot?" It seemed like a logical question.

"No," he answered, amused. "He designs things and writes. He told me he's working on some blueprints for some form of architecture. A building, I believe. He calls it the Umpire State Building. It seems Manuel was a baseball fan and never cared much for umpires. It's designed something like a dungeon."

"That's terrific!" Rosalie laughed, filling her mouth with popcorn, "really terrific!"

"Clever man, Manuel. He has a marvelous sense of humor." While settling into the sofa, Timothy slipped out of his shoes. "I hope you don't mind if I make myself comfortable."

"Heck, no. Make yourself at home."

She was growing more impatient by the minute, staring hard at the empty television screen. "What's the name of the show you said we're going to watch?"

"*This Is Your Life,*" Timothy replied, a sly look on his face.

"No kidding?" Rosalie perked up. "We used to watch that one back in Brooklyn when I was a kid. Not that I was crazy about it, mind you, but Mama liked to watch it. She had this pipe dream that maybe someday they would do her life. Like what had she ever done that would be interesting enough to put on television? Mama loved television. Nobody was even allowed to talk above a whisper when *The Lawrence Welk Show* came on Saturday nights. And Mama loved the soaps. She used to sit and watch with a box of tissues on her lap, blubbering and moaning about how life could be so cruel. She was a trip, my mother. And could she yell. Papa always said, 'We don't need a phone with you around. Just hang your head out the window—they'll hear you all the way to Jersey.' When I agreed with him, she usually hit me with a pillow. Something like that. Usually not too hard, then she would tell me not to be disrespectful to my elders. She was a nudge, my mother. You never heard the end of it."

Rosalie mimicked, "Marry a rich man, Rosalie! So you can take care of me when I'm old. Don't marry a bum like your father." Rosalie softly laughed while remembering her mother.

❀

"Was your father a bum?" Timothy inquired.

"Hell, no! Papa worked in a grocery store. That was where I learned how to be a checker. He wasn't a bum. He was just a plain, simple, hard-working man. It's just that Mama would have been happier if he had owned the store. Mama had a Jewish mother, too. All Jewish mothers want their daughters to marry rich men. It's inbred." She grew thoughtful.

"Mostly Papa was henpecked. Mama wore the pants in our family. She was liberated long before most women even thought about it." Her eyes misted over.

"Papa was kind, gentle, considerate—a simple man, and he loved the Talmud. He used to tell me funny stories and bring me hard apples from the store. I hate mushy apples. They give me the shivers."

"I've never cared much for soft apples myself, unless they're in a pie. I love apple pie," Timothy confessed.

"Me, too. A la mode with hot coffee and lots of cream and sugar in it. Now that's living!"

Timothy sighed. He couldn't help but wonder why someone like Rosalie had been called back so soon. She had died so young. There were still many aspects of Creation he had yet to understand. In time he hoped he would learn. Marcella claimed that eventually all souls would learn the Truth.

Irving suddenly let out a happy dog sigh. Then he rolled over onto his back, all four paws in the air with his head to one side, as dramatic music came from the television set. The large screen filled with brilliant golden light.

Rosalie pushed back on the arms of her recliner, making it recline. Her brown eyes lit up as the television screen filled with the words: THIS IS YOUR LIFE, fancy violet lettering on a brilliant white background. The music gave her goose bumps. A cold shiver rippled over her entire body, head to toe. She rubbed her arms to warm herself. A strange feeling in the pit of her stomach seemed to emerge from the very core of her being, dread mixed with anticipation. That was when she realized that it was *HER LIFE*.

For there on the television screen was a long, black limousine with David, Mama and Papa, Myrna, her mother-in-law, and Aunt Harriet inside. A long, black hearse followed the limousine. Inside the hearse was a light gray coffin covered with wreaths of flowers: yellow roses, pink roses, red roses, and white and yellow daisies from Honey, her best friend. Honey MacIntosh would never forget how much Rosalie Rosenberg loved daisies.

The experience Rosalie was having was unlike anything she had ever known. At times the room faded out, and she found herself with them in the limousine, and yet, at the same time, she was sitting in the den in her recliner viewing the montage before her. The effects were unique—heavenly special effects worth an Academy Award. Her eyes were fixed on the screen. Rosalie was holding her breath.

"Breathe," Timothy advised.

Rosalie let out a long, deep sigh. She didn't turn to look at him, for she was hypnotized by the scene before her. No other television show had ever held her interest like this one.

The funeral procession now arrived at Forest Lawn Cemetery, proceeding to an open grave site on a hillside near the statue of David—a copy of Michelangelo's work. Rosalie had always thought the sculpture was pretty nifty, even with the fig leaf. It left something to her imagination.

A Reformed rabbi was performing the rites. Funny how people get religious when somebody dies, Rosalie reflected. David was wearing a yarmulke and tallith—something he hadn't done since his father's funeral. The time before that was his bar mitzvah. There were tears in David's eyes. He didn't look so good. Rosalie was overwhelmed. Tears filled her eyes.

Mama looked old and bent, all dressed in black. Papa's shoulders were rounded, heavy, as he helped Mama to a chair beside the open grave. Rosalie was their only child.

An older brother had died at birth. Mama was told she should have no more children. It could kill her. It was her rheumatic heart. Mama was clutching a white handkerchief. So was Papa. Tears rolled down their sad faces. Papa was wearing a yarmulke and tallith, too. He rarely went to temple but Papa loved God and the Talmud.

David was wearing his navy blue suit, his last Christmas present from Rosalie. Forty-nine ninety-five at Forman and Clark's. They said it was marked down from a hundred and fifty. It looked nice on him. And he needed a suit. From the time Rosalie had moved to California and met Honey she celebrated Christmas along with Chanukah. Rosalie loved Christmas trees and Santa Claus. She was definitely goyish for a Jewish girl from Brooklyn. The family never approved, of course, but Rosalie didn't care. Mainly because Papa said he seriously doubted that it mattered to God one way or the other. Papa was such a good man, he had to know how God would feel about such things.

Rosalie and Honey taught David about Santa Claus and Christmas trees. He never objected. He was the one who put presents under the tree from Santa: bright, shiny things, inexpensive but funny or pretty. It made the holidays more fun for everyone.

Aunt Harriet looked the same as she always did, with her pinched mouth and rigid posture. Funerals were Aunt Harriet's style. She never missed one, even if she barely knew the person. At least she could mourn. People needed some kind of emotional outlet. If it couldn't be sex, or some kind of love, Rosalie guessed it might as well be grief. She had never once seen Aunt Harriet laugh. Poor Aunt Harriet. She was like the walking dead, all prim and proper in black crepe, carrying a white lace-trimmed handkerchief, her gray hair severely pulled back. Such a stereotypical old maid, Rosalie thought. No originality whatsoever. Naturally, she bought the dress especially for Rosalie's funeral. Aunt Harriet liked to think of herself as being Rosalie's *other mother*. She was Papa's older sister.

Papa's younger sister, Beatrice, had died of a heart attack at the age of fifty-two. Rosalie loved Aunt Beatrice. She was as fat and giving as Aunt Harriet was skinny and complaining. In Rosalie's eyes Aunt Beatrice was a wonderful woman. She had borne six children and raised them with tons of love. She married Uncle Irving when she was just sixteen. First love, last love. Uncle Irving and Aunt Beatrice were Rosalie's very favorite relatives. She loved them both dearly.

Cousin Solomon was their son. The one with a body like the statue of David. Since the biblical Solomon was the son of David, to Rosalie it made sense. And this Solomon had a harem, too, just like the one in the bible. He was working on his third marriage, with a mistress to boot. Solomon practiced law in Miami. He was only six years older than Rosalie, and her death had truly upset him. But Solomon hated funerals. For that reason he decided not to come.

Another young man arrived at the graveside. He sat in the empty chair near Aunt Harriet.

"What do you know! It's my cousin, Herbie! The one Irving saved from the German shepherd. Look, Irving! You saved his life, and there he is!"

Irving simply rolled over and closed his eyes again. After all, Herbie had changed. He was thirty now, a bit pudgy with a receding hairline. He was only a kid when Irving saved his life, and people change a lot more than dogs do.

"Herbie will repay Irving by helping another," Timothy volunteered.

But Rosalie wasn't listening. Honey MacIntosh had just sat down next to Myrna Rosenberg, David's mother. Imagine Myrna allowing a Gentile to sit next to her at a Jewish funeral. Myrna was the most prejudiced, non-religious Jewish mother Rosalie had ever met. She acted like she considered herself among the chosen after David's father died, which made her the official head of the family.

Next, David's brother, Kenny, and his wife, Nancy, arrived. She was six months pregnant with their third child.

Everyone hoped it would be a boy. They already had two girls. No one else showed up. That was it, ten people, including the rabbi. Not a big funeral. It was how the family wanted it, small and simple. It had been such an awful shock. Rosalie was so young and healthy. No one expected her to fall off a roof and die. David had killed the television set, and the antenna. He swore he would never own another one, an obvious overreaction. The television set was innocent enough. Rosalie wondered why he hadn't killed the crow. And she knew in her heart that for the rest of his life David Rosenberg would never climb up on a roof under any circumstances whatsoever. Her death had done nothing to improve his acrophobia.

The rabbi intoned a prayer in Hebrew, which was totally lost on Rosalie. She only knew a few words, mostly slang, but it gave her a nice feeling. Then David stood up beside the rabbi. He was crying, silently. During the four years of their marriage Rosalie had only seen David cry twice—the day his father died and the day his father was buried. David loved and truly respected his father. But now, David just stood there. He stared at the casket suspended over the open grave, covered with flowers and ribbons. The wreath of red roses had a white satin ribbon with silver lettering: *My Beloved Wife, Rosalie.*

Tears began to roll down Rosalie's cheeks, and she quietly began to sob. Timothy pulled a handkerchief from his pocket and handed it to her. This kind of scene always got to him, too. He pulled out another for himself and began to dab at his eyes.

"The Lord is my shepherd," David began, his voice starting to break, "I shall not want. He maketh me to lie down in green pastures; he leadeth me beside the still waters. He restoreth my soul; he leadeth me in the paths of righteousness for his name's sake. Yea, though I walk through the valley of the shadow of death, I will fear no evil, for thou art with me; thy rod and thy staff they comfort me. Thou preparest a table before me in the presence of mine enemies; thou anointest my head with oil; my cup runneth over. Surely goodness and mercy shall follow me all the days of my life, and I will dwell in the house of the Lord forever."

By the end of the prayer, David was crying like a baby. Then he began beating his chest. The Jew in him was coming out in full force. It could have been the Wailing Wall.

"David, what are you doing to yourself?" Rosalie cried out in horror. "I'm okay, David! Really! I'm fine."

But David's wailing continued. His hands now covered his face as he sobbed.

"David, stop it. I'm alive, David. I'm alive!"

But David couldn't hear her as he fell to his knees, crying his heart out. Now Papa joined him. He was carrying on, too, and Mama was beginning to wail like a banshee. Everybody was blubbering, moaning, sobbing, and carrying on. Even Honey, who was Scotch-Irish.

"Stop it, will you?" Rosalie leaped out of her chair and ran to the television. At the same time she could feel herself there in the cemetery and here in Lakeside in front of the television set, being pulled back and forth, in and out, while she cried out, "Please stop it! Please!"

Yet still no one heard her.

"Please stop!" she pleaded, reaching out, unable to touch them. All at once, she didn't know whether to laugh or to cry. It all seemed so ridiculous.

"I'm okay, folks. I'm alive and living in Lakeside," she told them, laughing and crying at the same time. "I have a beautiful home and an adorable dog and a gardener from the Bronx. I have a friend named Timothy, who's terrific, and a swimming pool and a Jacuzzi and everything. Stop it, will you? You're breaking my heart. Please! You're all going to make yourselves sick." Rosalie was in torment.

"There is no death," she explained, tears flowing. She tried to reach out to David, Mama and Papa, Aunt Harriet, Honey, and everyone else lamenting her loss.

"It's like taking a trip and not telling anyone where you went or why you left, that's all!" She helplessly sat down on the floor, watching them, fearful that they would never stop crying.

"You all need to understand that dying is like having your birthday everyday," she nearly shouted to make herself heard. Then in desperation, she turned to Timothy. "This is awful, Timothy. There they are, carrying on, and here I am, perfectly fine. I'm not in that box. I'm not there, and they can't even hear me. They don't understand, Timothy. They just don't understand."

"It's true, lass," he agreed. "They don't understand. Many souls can't see the truth—not for the life of them."

"That's shitty, Timothy! Real shitty!" she cried out, while Timothy attempted to control his energy field.

"Goddamn, Timothy, they deserve to know that I'm all right!" Rosalie got to her feet and started to pace.

"Grief is not for those who have gone on. It is for those left behind to cope in their limited reality," he assured her as his heart went out to her.

"But I'm not dead!" she shouted. "I know I'm not dead, and you know I'm not dead. Why can't they know?"

"You are dead to their dimension of awareness. They live within the obstructed universe. They must learn to expand and grow beyond the limitations of earth. All souls will one day. It's the Plan, lass. Eventually all conscious souls will expand and grow. I'm afraid I don't have a better explanation for you right now."

Rosalie sat staring at the television scene with a pained expression on her face. Her family and friends were beginning to regain some semblance of self-control. They were starting to walk away from the grave. David walked between her parents, a comforting arm around each one. They needed one another, all three of them. The others straggled behind. Only Honey lingered near the casket, watching, as two men lowered it into the freshly dug grave.

As the gray rectangular box descended, Honey picked up a handful of earth, tossing it in on top of the casket. Her eyes were red from crying. Tears still rolled down her cheeks.

Too bad she couldn't lose twenty-five pounds, Rosalie mused. Her face was pretty, even though it was covered with freckles, like most strawberry blondes Rosalie had known. Honey's green eyes were sprinkled with golden flecks. She looked one hundred percent Irish. She had been baptized Roman Catholic as a baby, but had stopped going to church at the age of twelve. That was when the priest told her that reading tea leaves was the work of the devil. She had never trusted a Catholic priest since. Honey had always been able to see things in the tea leaves—strange, wonderful, interesting things that happened in the future. It all started when she was five.

Such a strange girl, Rosalie thought. *Beware the ides of March and raven's wings* echoed in her mind as Rosalie sat forward to say to Honey, "Why in hell didn't you just tell me not to climb on the roof in the month of March? A fine friend you were!"

A strange look formed in Honey's eyes. The kind of look she always got when she read tea leaves. She quickly looked around, halfway expecting to see Rosalie standing there— or someone, anyone. Then she shivered from head to toe, rubbing her arms with her hands to take away the chill. It was a blustery March day, dark and overcast. Soon it would rain. Honey got a strange feeling right in middle of her solar plexus. Again she shivered. She wondered if she might be catching cold. In her left hand was a single white rosebud with a sprig of baby's breath. As moist earth was shoveled onto the casket, Honey tossed the flowers into the grave, whispering, "Good-bye, dear friend. Rest well." Then she quickly turned to walk back down the hill in a different direction from the others, who were now climbing into the limousine. Honey didn't feel like sharing their grief. At that moment she wanted to be alone.

David, Myrna, Mama and Papa, and Aunt Harriet were all again seated in the limo. All of them were sniffling, mopping wet noses with wet handkerchiefs. Rosalie was overcome with a deep sense of sadness.

"It makes me feel terrible. There they are miserable, and here I am just fine."

"One day they will understand, lass," Timothy assured her. "It just takes time."

"Why does it have to be like this?" The emotion had drained her.

"Most of us cannot evolve when we have foreknowledge. That is a privilege earned by those with a mission to teach the rest. When most souls enter the earth plane they drink from the vial of forgetfulness. It's necessary in order for them to develop and grow. That's as much as I can tell you at this point."

Rosalie stared at her loved ones, alone in their grief. She had never realized how much David had loved her. He was like a lost little boy. He had never been close to his mother. Now they were touching, drawn together by mutual loss. David's father had died the year David married Rosalie. He had always said his father was a good and considerate man—just like her Papa.

"It all seems so senseless," David was saying.

"Nothing makes sense in this world," Aunt Harriet muttered.

Wasn't it just like Aunt Harriet to be cheerful at a time like this? David simply shook his head, a numbed expression on his face. David had always been more tolerant of her Aunt Harriet than Rosalie had ever been.

Mama was resting her head on Papa's shoulder. He was gently stroking her hair. Poor Mama. Her only child was gone. Papa was being strong. He believed in God. He believed God knew what he was doing. Thank God for that. Mama could lean on him now. Maybe she would stop bossing him around so much. On the other hand, Papa was used to her bossing him around. He wouldn't know how to act if she stopped, especially after thirty-five years.

Rosalie could feel their warmth, their love for her. It was beautiful. She could also feel their anguish. That wasn't beautiful. That was hell.

Back at the funeral home people got into their separate cars. David had rented a blue Toyota. Mama and Papa rode with him. They had flown in from New York just yesterday. Rosalie never thought her parents would fly in an airplane for any reason at all. Rosalie's funeral was a reason. It was their first plane trip. Mama had been scared to death. She had taken a tranquilizer, but she liked flying after all. She drank a lot of ginger ale on the plane. Papa thought the flight attendant was pretty. He enjoyed the flight.

Naturally Mama didn't like going to Rosalie's funeral. Mama hated funerals. Papa didn't hate them but he wasn't crazy about them either. Papa's heart was heavy. His *Rozele* had gone to the bosom of Abraham, Isaac, and Jacob. For all he knew, she was talking to Moses right now.

"You're hardly Moses," Rosalie responded, turning to Timothy, who smiled in agreement.

"I'll be damned!" she exclaimed. "I just read Papa's thoughts!" She was excited. "I mean, I did read his thoughts, didn't I?"

"I told you that you'd be doing it too in no time. A bit unnerving, isn't it, lass?" He looked pleased.

"No, it's great!" She was so pleased. "How about that? Peeking into other people's minds." She turned to the television, admitting, "Papa, I haven't met Moses or Abraham, Isaac or Jacob. I've only met Timothy O'Toole and Manuel Sierra. But you'd like them, Papa. Honest, you would. They're both terrific!"

Irving sat up, stretched and yawned, his tongue hanging out.

"And Irving," she added, patting the dog on the head. "You may not remember him, Papa. Although I don't see how anyone could forget Irving, and how he saved Herbie's life." She smiled a sad smile, her love for her father flowing out from her in waves.

Papa's expression suddenly changed. His spirits seemed to lift. He got this distinct feeling that his Rosalie was all right. The crisis was over. At least she had gone quickly. She had never known what hit her. It was all over in one big blow.

"It's true, Papa. So true," she told him. "I couldn't even remember what had happened when I got here."

Reading thoughts was really fun. Now she turned her attention to David, drawing an absolute blank.

"You can't always expect to score a hundred percent on your first try," Timothy consoled. "Perhaps another time. For the moment, I think you've had quite enough food for thought."

"Is it like this for everyone?" She felt limp, exhausted.

"It's different for each of us every time."

For the time being she didn't want to explore the possibilities implied by his remark. His words brought up too many questions. Instead, she just stared at the now blank television screen.

She had discovered that she had been loved. Truly loved. She felt lucky. Too bad she hadn't realized how much everyone loved her when she was there with them, she thought. If she had, perhaps things would have been different. Nevertheless, it felt good to know. She guessed it was never too late to find out that you're loved. It was sort of like finding out that you're alive when everyone thinks that you're dead and you're not.

Rosalie just sat there, searching her mind. She was wondering whether there was some way to let them all know that she was fine, really fine, happy even. After all, it had worked with Papa. There had to be a way to let the others know, too—to let David know. With God's help, she would find the way. ✻

Chapter Nine

That night Rosalie's sleep was not dreamless. She dreamt herself into the past, reviewing her life, remembering—remembering—remembering. Assorted scenes moved in a montage before her mind's eye, somewhat disconnected yet with continuity of purpose. Important events from her childhood were dramatically interspersed with memories of her more recent adult life with David. They had been married for four years. To her way of thinking, she'd been an old maid when she married him—twenty-five.

Mama thought she would never get married. But then, Rosalie had never told Mama about Harlan Meitzloff or Sidney Sylvestan. Mama was old-fashioned. She would have considered her daughter a fallen woman. Aunt Harriet would have fainted. Rosalie seriously doubted whether Aunt Harriet had ever even been kissed, really kissed. But then, who would have wanted to kiss her? Aunt Harriet was a Virgo, and to Rosalie's way of thinking, the worst kind. Too bad Aunt Harriet wasn't more like Elizabeth the First. Now that would have been interesting.

Rosalie reviewed her times with Aunt Beatrice and Uncle Irving and all her crazy cousins—happy days filled with laughter. There had been a special kind of madness. There were the days when Aunt Beatrice cooked those wonderful, delicious meals. Aunt Beatrice was a fabulous cook. She made the best matzo-ball soup. And there were the Sunday brunches complete with cream cheese, lox, and bagels. Pickled herring Rosalie wasn't crazy about, but Uncle Irving loved it. He could eat a quart. His waistline showed it.

The Uncle Irving Rosalie had known had never been slender—he'd been barrel-chested and bay-bellied. Aunt Beatrice had the biggest bosom in the family, so soft to cuddle up against when Rosalie was small. Aunt Beatrice was always nice and soft and round. When she laughed, her whole body shook. She had a real laugh, an honest, sincere laugh. Everybody loved Aunt Beatrice. She was a loving, lovable woman. Her only weakness was food. Aunt Beatrice loved to eat, and she loved to cook. She ate what she cooked. Why not? It was delicious.

And Uncle Irving, he could be gruff sometimes, but everyone knew not to take him seriously. Uncle Irving was a pussycat, and so tender-hearted—especially with all the girls. They had four daughters: Karen, Catherine, Susan, and Dorothy. Susan was Rosalie's age. She wore braces until she was sixteen years old but it paid off. She married a doctor, an obstetrician. They had a beautiful home in Chatham, New Jersey, two children, and two poodles. They went to Israel last summer, then Paris and Rome. Susan got pinched in Italy. She said she always knew she would. They always sent postcards from wherever they went on vacation. That way the rest of the family knew that they were doing okay. All of the Taylor girls had done okay. None of them had married a vacuum cleaner salesman. Their husbands were professional men. They each had their own home, big houses with gardens and lawns. And they had kids running around, two each. They had real honest-to-goodness families.

Aunt Beatrice's youngest son, Solomon, had three wives and nine children. He had two exes, each with three kids. Now his third wife was pregnant with their fourth. That made ten kids. Solomon could afford it. He was making a fortune dealing in accident cases in Miami. Besides, Solomon was too handsome for his own good. Women were just crazy about him. He had a mistress, plus a couple girlfriends. Face it, Solomon was a ladies' man. The family figured since he had had three wives by the time he was thirty-five, it was anybody's guess how many wives and children he would accumulate during his entire life. The prospects were amazing. They thought he sure was living up to his name on that score.

But Uncle Irving had never been totally happy with Solomon. He claimed they never should have given him the name. He always said he had hoped the name would make him wise instead of a damn fool. Yet everyone knew Solomon was a good lawyer. He did use his brains for something besides screwing. And besides, Uncle Irving knew that not just any man could find a good woman like his Beatrice.

Such love those two had for each other—love you could feel. Uncle Irving didn't mind that Aunt Beatrice was fat. He said it just gave him that much more to love. All the time they hugged and they kissed. He never remarried after Beatrice died. He planted flowers on her grave, new ones every spring. He paid the caretaker extra to see that the flowers were properly watered and cared for. That was enduring love—love that continued to flower and bloom.

David gave Rosalie flowers on their second date. Violets. They cost him a dollar. David never did have much money. No guy had ever given her flowers before. She put them in a jelly glass on her dresser. They lasted a whole week.

The day after David proposed to Rosalie he sent her long-stemmed red roses. He had never bought her red roses again until the funeral. She had made him feel too guilty about spending the money. After all, they were supposed to be saving for their future. If she had known the future would only last four years, she might have reconsidered. Rosalie saved the roses in a cigar box. She had to cut off most of the stems to make them fit, but she saved all twelve roses, along with the card that read: *I love you, my Rosalie. Yours Forever, David.*

When he was sorting through her things in the top of the closet, David found the dead roses and his card in the cigar box. It made him cry—for hours. He'd never realized that Rosalie was so sentimental. Tears now rolled down Rosalie's cheeks as she dreamed. There is so much we don't see or understand. We are all too eager to blame and find fault. She was learning something about mortal blindness, the kind experienced by people with 20/20 vision.

Rosalie and David had met in the grocery store. He had forgotten his wallet and didn't realize it until she rang up twenty-four dollars and sixty-five cents for food and detergent. David really needed the groceries and was more annoyed with himself than embarrassed. Rosalie trusted him to take the groceries home. After all, he promised to bring back the money. The manager nearly fired her right before David came back, just like he said he would, all smiles and apologies. He explained everything to the manager, who still insisted that she should have kept the groceries there in the store. But Rosalie just knew from the looks of him that David had to be a nice, honest Jewish boy, and besides that, she thought he was kind of cute.

After David paid the bill, he nearly left without asking for her phone number. He was selling encyclopedias then. Britannica. Not too many people were buying. He did a lot better with vacuum cleaners.

They discovered that they only lived three blocks apart. It was convenient to ask her out. He could walk. Besides, he found her refreshing, naive. How could she possibly know he would come back with the money? And besides, she was a cute girl, and she was Jewish. Rosalie Resnick. But could she ever talk! She asked him one crazy question after another. And was she funny! Maybe not the smartest girl in the whole world, but at least grocery checkers made a decent living. She was no Jewish princess like Kathy, the girl he used to date.

❧

Kathy's mother made David uncomfortable. She wore diamond rings on three fingers and claimed wives shouldn't work. That made David nervous. After all, he was planning on being another Ernest Hemingway, or maybe John Steinbeck. Writers didn't make that much money when they were starting out. Neither did encyclopedia salesmen. Kathy's father had his own business, a clothing store in Culver City. He offered David a job. That made David even more nervous. David wasn't into readywear. It just wasn't his thing.

Besides, grocery checkers could add and subtract. He thought maybe that Rosalie could help him to balance his accounts. She did. She made herself indispensable. Rosalie was no dummy. Besides, David was so charming and so lovable, even if he didn't have money. And he was quiet. Not that he always listened. Sometimes he tuned her out. Like when she nagged or got domineering or demanding. It was something that his father had taught him about women. Most of the time it worked.

David also thought Rosalie was a little bit crazy. Most of the time she seemed illogical, just like most of the women he had known. But she was funny, very funny. Every day they laughed. David realized that Rosalie's craziness somehow balanced his extreme sense of caution. He realized that with Rosalie life would never be dull. But mostly, he realized that he loved her. Love wasn't logical. Love was Rosalie. It took five months for David to realize that. That was when he decided to propose.

"Why don't we move into one apartment instead of keeping up two? It's practical," he said, his heart beating in his throat, small beads of perspiration starting to form on his upper lip.

"So what are you trying to say, David?" Rosalie inquired, and she wasn't smiling.

"We could live together," he tried to sound offhand, but knew he wasn't quite making it. Now he was really beginning to sweat.

"Do you know what that would do to my mother, David? My mother would have a heart attack and die." Still she wasn't smiling. "Do you want my mother to have a heart attack and die? Is that what you want, David?"

David tried to smile. It wasn't easy. He was twenty-six and broke. Marriage seemed so permanent, so binding.

"Well, I guess we could get married," he ventured, amazed the words had actually come out of his mouth. Inwardly he was convinced that the really good writers just lived with women. They were wild, carefree. What about his career? His future? What in the hell was he doing to himself?

"Do you really want to marry me, David?" Now she was smiling.

It had sounded more like resignation than a proposal, but no other guy she had ever known had even come close to saying those words, asking that question, except Peter Watson in sixth grade, and he was a geek.

A sheepish smile played on David's lips. He was doomed. He sheepishly nodded. "Why not! I love you, Rosalie."

"I love you, too, David. And if I can't marry you for your money, which you don't have, I guess I might as well marry you for love, which you seem to have plenty of!"

They fell into bed and made love for hours, then slept through the night like contented children. They were married a month later in a small civil ceremony. David's mother objected. Rosalie's mother was relieved. Her daughter had finally fulfilled her main purpose in life—at least the first. Next there would be grandchildren. They had never told Mama that they didn't want kids right away. Kids would come later, after David finished his book.

Four years later David was still writing his book. It was almost finished. He was still trying, very hard. But now Rosalie was gone. There would be no children. David was now a widower with an unborn book, and no wife for whom to labor. There was no one to read his story to now. No one to argue with about the characters or plot. No one was there to encourage him to write the very next chapter. David was beginning to wonder whether his book, like their child, would also never be born.

Pieces in the puzzle of her life slowly began to fit into place, one by one. Misunderstandings, unrealistic expectations, hopes, dreams, desires, aspirations, partial realities and unknown factors all got in the way of fulfillment. She saw David's tears, his fears and frustrations. His hopes dashed. His need to have someone to be successful for. David was devastated by her death but not completely broken. He blamed himself for his fears, for not paying attention to his intuition, for not making her life a bed of roses. So she nagged him. It was a family tradition. His mother had nagged him. Why not Rosalie? The nagging was not so bad, really. It usually went in one ear and out the other.

Business had been bad due to inflation. People just weren't buying that many vacuum cleaners. And besides, David really hated selling. He wanted to finish his book but there were just not enough hours in the day. And then, Rosalie had always had jobs waiting for him, a hundred zillion ideas about what should be done to the house. She had talked about all the grand and glorious things they would buy someday. That made David nervous. Maybe Rosalie was a Jewish princess after all. How could he possibly afford all of those things?

David had never understood that in her heart it didn't really matter. That it was mostly talk. Rosalie didn't really mind just pretending. After all, her mother and grandmother had pretended for a long time before her. Mortal blindness, a common disease usually detected too late. If David had only known just how much roses had meant to Rosalie, he would have sent her roses everyday. Let her yell and scream about the money. He loved her. On their last anniversary he had given her yellow daisies. He found them pressed in a

scrapbook with other mementos from their time together—
her secret scrapbook—like her secret cigar box. She was just
a woman after all.

From that time on, whenever David Rosenberg saw red
roses or yellow daisies he would think of Rosalie and he
would remember, sadness mixed with love. Memories that
make you bleed a little, but blood is warm. Blood is life. Life
is filled with remembering. He would keep the scrapbook
and cigar box in his own secret place forever. Someday he
might even write about it. But the girl would not fall off a
roof. That wouldn't be romantic. A fatal disease would be
much better. Who cared that it had already been done?

Bits and pieces of her life flowed through the passage-
ways of her mind. Mama and Papa. Aunt Harriet. Aunt
Beatrice. Aunt Sarah. Her life in Brooklyn. Her life in California. Memories that opened her mind, her consciousness.
She became aware of her lethargy, her indifference, and her
enthusiasm. Her capacity and incapacity to love. She
struggled with her curiosity, kindness, and caring, as well as
the honesty and lies that had been a part of her life. Her soul
resolutely revealed the virtues and the vices that had been
an integral part of her life.

At times Rosalie's sleep was peaceful and calm, other
times restless, fitful, distressed. She was continuing to learn,
to grow, and to develop within the very depths of her soul.
She was becoming more alive. More aware. More complete.
More whole. She was sleeping yet not sleeping. Dreaming
yet living. Remembering the life of a girl named Rosalie. A
girl she had been. A girl she was still. She was her, yet not
her. She was watching, observing, and taking stock—balanc-
ing the ledger of her life. ✳

Chapter Ten

It was another morning in eternity. Sunshine filtered through the windowpanes. Birds sang. A gentle breeze ruffled the transparent curtains. The smell of coffee perking and bacon frying drifted up from the kitchen. Rosalie's family had never been kosher. She loved bacon almost as much as she loved popcorn. Especially crisp bacon with the fat all cooked.

The smell of breakfast helped clear the sleep from her head. For a moment she just lay there gazing up at the green canopy overhead. Irving was curled up on the corner of the bed, watching her. He seemed to smile. Upon realizing Rosalie was fully awake, he raised up on his hind legs and stretched, tail wagging in anticipation.

Her memory of her night's dream drifted hazily through her mind, mostly in essence. The image of David stood out the strongest. Dear, sweet David. So what if his ears stuck out a little. They were good ears. And Honey was right. He was handsome. He might not be an Adonis, but his body was anything but repulsive. He was tall and lean. A little skinny, maybe, but Rosalie had never been attracted to fat men.

Their sex life had been damn good at times. What do you want, the Fourth of July every time? There hadn't really been that much time for sex towards the end. David was always working or going to school—or writing. Rosalie knew they couldn't screw all the time. Uncle Irving always said that Solomon screwed so much that one of these days his brain would fall out of his groin. Sometimes Uncle Irving could be crude but funny.

The tinkling bell sounded from downstairs—the kind of bell Aunt Beatrice always rang on weekends back in Trenton when breakfast was ready. Rosalie sat up. Again the bell rang. Rosalie's face lit up. She leaped out of bed and ran down the stairs. The woman standing in the kitchen looked to be about thirty-five. She was pleasingly plump, not fat. She wore a floral print housedress and a clean, white apron.

"I thought you were going to sleep all day," she said, a broad smile on her face.

"Aunt Beatrice?" Rosalie rubbed her eyes and stared hard. It had to be Aunt Beatrice, but she was a mere shadow of her former self.

It was then that the woman threw her head back in a hearty peal of laughter. It was Aunt Beatrice all right. They fell upon each other with kisses and hugs and hugs and kisses. Aunt Beatrice still had the biggest, softest bosom in the family. Tears of joy freely rolled down their faces.

"Look at you! Just look at you! How pretty you are!" Aunt Beatrice declared, taking Rosalie's tear-stained face in her hands. "What a face! Oh, my goodness, what a face!"

"Oh, Aunt Beatrice, you're alive!" Rosalie sobbed. "I'm so glad. Really I am."

"Now, now," she replied, comforting her while leading Rosalie to the breakfast table where bacon, eggs, hash browns, toast, orange juice and coffee were waiting. "Eat some breakfast. You'll feel better. You could stand a little meat on your bones."

The two women stared at each other in wonder. Love waves filled the room. Again they embraced, hugging for dear life. The memories they shared were sweet.

"In a while, we'll have company. Some friends are coming, Timothy and Manuel," she announced, using her apron to wipe away her tears. "Drink some coffee. Eat your eggs.

You'll feel better. I fixed them the way you like them. Sort of mushy."

While staring down at the food on the table, Rosalie shook her head. It was just like back in Trenton. "The way Uncle Irving likes them," Rosalie sniffled. "He's the one who taught me how to eat eggs."

"I know," Aunt Beatrice beamed, and they both sat down at the table and stared at the eggs. "He can't eat so many now, you know. It's his cholesterol. Bad for his heart. He's a stubborn man, your Uncle Irving. Such a stubborn man. I keep telling him, let up on the eggs and pickled herring, but does he listen? He doesn't listen. He goes right on making a glutton of himself. And one of these days that old heart of his is going to give out on him just like mine did, and he's going to wake up and find himself here. And believe me, when he does, am I ever going to give him what for! Who is he to be so stubborn, I ask you?"

Rosalie knew that she was just getting started. The pattern was all so familiar.

"He's a young man, my Irving," Aunt Beatrice continued, "and his family needs him. There's plenty for him to do there, yet. Grandchildren for him to raise with love. That upstart of a Solomon to scream at. What's a mother to do? I keep trying to tell him, stop watering the lilies, Irving. Spend more time with your children and grandchildren, but does he listen?" She shook her head.

"He doesn't listen," Rosalie replied, shaking her head in agreement.

"He's a stubborn man," they chimed in unison. Then they grinned and laughed until they nearly cried.

"Eat your eggs," Aunt Beatrice prompted, a smile on her face. "You'll feel better."

Rosalie picked up a fork and started eating her eggs. It did make her feel better. Aunt Beatrice was always right. Everything tasted so good, the way it used to back home. The bacon was just right. There was orange marmalade for the toast, the kind Aunt Beatrice used to can back in Jersey.

While eating breakfast, the women watched each other, fond love in their eyes. They were trying to digest their re-union along with the food.

"You had no business climbing up on roofs, you know," Aunt Beatrice chided. "A big girl like you climbing on roofs. When I heard about it, I nearly died! You always were such a daredevil. I remember. Believe me, Rosalie. I remember."

"What do you mean you nearly died?" Rosalie asked, swallowing a mouthful of coffee.

"It's a figure of speech. So sue me!" She pushed herself away from the table and narrowed her eyes. "At first I wanted to spank you good. But then I realized what good would it do me? Or you, for that matter? Your time was up. So you fell off a roof. Big deal. I ate myself to death and died of a heart attack, like your Uncle Irving's going to do, too, if he doesn't watch out."

"It's Stanley I worry about, and your poor mother. Your Papa's taken this badly. You were his sunshine. His pride and joy. His *Rozele!* My poor brother, such a good man he is," she declared, covering another piece of toast with mar-malade.

"You look so young, Aunt Beatrice." Rosalie was charmed by the vision in front of her. "I mean, you look better than I ever saw you. Honest, you look terrific. Really terrific!"

"I've been around awhile. I've had time to look better. You don't need time to look better. You look better already," she declared, laughing her loving laugh. "You look so pretty, so fresh, so young." Her expression became more serious. "I'm still on a diet, you know. Nothing changes. Here, it's easier, but not at first. At first it's harder. It takes time to get easier."

"Do you live here in Lakeside, too?"

"Me? Good heavens, no!" Aunt Beatrice started to clear away the dirty dishes, an old habit. "I live in Seaside. You know how Uncle Irving and I were always going to retire in

❧

Miami to be near Solomon and his expanding brood. Well, I live in a mobile home in Seaside. It's something like Miami but the people are nicer. No snobs or uppity types hanging around there. In fact, a lot of my relatives are there, too. A few you might even remember, but most came here long before you were born.

"It's nice where I live. Blue skies, clean air, palm trees, white sand beaches, dolphins that play with the children in the surf. It's heaven, Rosalie. You'll like it. You must come and see me sometime real soon."

"Why don't you move in with me here? I have plenty of room," Rosalie enthusiastically suggested. Heaven surely would include Aunt Beatrice's cooking.

Aunt Beatrice thoughtfully shook her head before answering, "No, *Rozele*. This isn't for me. This is your place. I have my own. You'll see. Then you'll understand. And we can visit each other any time we like. It's allowed."

Rosalie thoughtfully finished her coffee as Aunt Beatrice cleared the table. She was beginning to see things more clearly for the first time—fine points in a greater reality.

"You will visit me again? You're very important to me, Aunt Beatrice." Rosalie's eyes filled with loving gratitude.

"You just try and keep me away," she said. "I'll come and see you whenever you like, and you can come and visit me in Seaside. We have mineral baths. They're terrific. You'll like them."

She poured more coffee into their cups, then looked into Rosalie's eyes. "You turned out to be a real beauty, Rosalie." She tenderly brushed Rosalie's cheek with her fingertips, "You're such a pretty girl!"

"Oh, Aunt Beatrice, you've got something in your eye."

"I always told you that you were beautiful, and you are. It's the truth. So shush your mouth and learn to say thank you. You never did know how to accept a compliment. So learn, already!" Aunt Beatrice was smiling again.

"I'll learn, I'll learn," Rosalie replied. "Thank you, already!"

Rosalie couldn't get over the way Aunt Beatrice had changed. Before she died she had been extremely overweight. Her hair was gray and her face filled with lines. Now she was just slightly plump and her hair was chestnut brown. Her skin was smooth and pink. She looked young, so pretty. The way she looked in the old photograph albums in the old pine cupboard in the family room. When she was a kid growing up in Brooklyn, Rosalie always loved looking at those photographs. Aunt Beatrice and Uncle Irving were always ready to tell the stories that went with the pictures of all the different relatives in the extended family. All their kids loved to look at the pictures, too.

"I think you're beautiful, too, Aunt Beatrice," Rosalie told her. "I always did think you were beautiful, and now that I see you like this, well, I can see where all the girls got their looks. Let's face it, Aunt Beatrice, Uncle Irving is no Miss America."

"My Irving is all right," she defended. "He was a humdinger of a young man, Rosalie. So dashing! So debonair! So good to me you wouldn't believe. And such a lover! No wonder my Solomon is such a mess. It's his father's genes. My Irving put all of his eggs in one basket, but not my Solomon. He's out to screw the world. He thinks he's the only bee in the garden, and he has to pollinate all the flowers single-handedly, yet! He'll be lucky he doesn't wear it out before he's fifty, God help him."

"Now, my Daniel, he's more like his Papa." she was talking about her other son, her eldest child.

"Danny's a nice enough guy," Rosalie was forced to agree. "Danny is very respectable and responsible. He should make you proud. He's getting bald."

"Like his Papa! Just like my Irving," she was overjoyed. "He looks like his Papa, too. Such a nice boy he is, my Danny boy."

Death had not changed Aunt Beatrice, not at all. She looked younger and more radiant, even more alive. But she was the same good-natured, kind-hearted, loving woman, totally concerned with her husband and family. So she lived someplace like Miami. Nice, Rosalie thought. If anyone she had ever known deserved a bit of heaven it was Aunt Beatrice. For she had spent the better part of her life seeing that other people enjoyed and tasted just a little bit of heaven.

"So how did you know how to find me?" Rosalie felt the need to ask.

"News gets around. Actually, it was Irving."

"Uncle Irving?" Rosalie was amazed. "But how?"

"We talk, you know," she said as a soft light formed in her eyes. "He tells me what's going on there, and I try to let him know I'm doing okay. I keep telling him, stop watering the lilies. I'm not there yet. I'm here in Seaside. But does he listen?"

"He doesn't listen," they again said in unison, then laughed. "He's a stubborn man!"

"You really have visits?" Rosalie was fascinated.

"All the time," Beatrice revealed. "And he told me that I should look after you, make you feel welcome. Like he has to tell me, already. Such a bossy man, my Irving. A good man he is, but bossy." She shook her head as a faraway look formed in her eyes.

"Now you go get dressed before your friends get here and find you in your nightgown. Go on, " she admonished.

Rosalie drained the last drop of coffee from her cup. Dying was certainly interesting. She was learning so much. So they talked, Aunt Beatrice and Uncle Irving. They had visits. Even though he was on earth and she was here. Maybe she could talk to David. Or Mama and Papa. Or Honey. It had seemed like Papa had heard her. At least he stopped crying and grieving so much. It made him get quiet inside. The prospects were exciting. Aunt Beatrice had given her valuable insight.

When she stood up, Rosalie gave Aunt Beatrice a big hug. "Thanks for being here, Aunt Beatrice." She quickly caught herself and felt the need to apologize, "Not that I'm glad that you died!"

"I just took a vacation," Beatrice informed her as she turned Rosalie toward the stairs. "So go get dressed. Put on something pretty for your friends. You'll feel better. And get a move on, already."

"You know something, you haven't changed a bit," Rosalie called over her shoulder as she obediently ran for the stairs.

"So what did you expect—a miracle? So I'm a little skinnier. Big deal! And I look younger. Bigger deal! A Beatrice is a Beatrice and I'm a Beatrice. That's the way I'm made, and that's the way it is."

Aunt Beatrice was talking to herself. It was a family trait, inbred. As she finished rinsing the dishes, there was a knock at the kitchen door.

"Since when do you need an invitation?" she called out.

And Timothy and Manuel walked into the kitchen. Manuel had on a patchwork shirt and was wearing sneakers with his blue jeans. Timothy looked less like a leprechaun. He was slimmer and his clothes were much more modern.

"And how are you this fine day, Father O'Toole?" Beatrice had a broad smile on her face.

"Just fine, thank you. I'm sure Rosalie was delighted to find you here."

"Such a beauty, my *Rozele*. What a face! So young to cross over, but here she is. The least I can do is make her feel welcome. She always did like my cooking, even though she eats like a bird."

Beatrice frowned. "My poor brother, Stanley, two children he had. One dies at birth and the other falls off a roof at twenty-nine, childless, leaving a fine man like David to go crazy with grief. I tell you—sometimes I don't understand the way they run things around here, but who am I, I ask you? I guess they know what they're doing, but sometimes I wonder."

Manuel was taking in her essence. Nice lady, he thought, good at heart and really sweet.

"You must be Manuel," Beatrice said in a teasing tone, giving him a quick once-over. "What a looker!"

"You're not so bad yourself," he countered with a smile. "So you're Aunt Beatrice. I had a cousin named Beatrice in Puerto Rico."

"I've never been to Puerto Rico," was her flat reply.

"Me neither, but I always wanted to go and see the fortress in old San Juan."

"I hear they have lovely churches there, too," Timothy chimed in.

"Ancient Spanish cathedrals."

"Is that right?"

"Oh, yeah!" Manuel informed him. "The Catholics are big in Puerto Rico. You'd like it there."

Timothy blushed. He had hoped the absence of his collar would alter his image somewhat. Manuel was the only Catholic he had met in that dimension and Manuel had never practiced Catholicism when he was grown. But he had attended Catholic schools. Timothy was slowly realizing that it was time for him to relate to himself simply as a soul operating under the masculine principle. When he returned to earth he somehow knew that he would be a man again, with the priesthood a thing of the past.

"I hear tell you're taking my Rosalie to a country fair?" Aunt Beatrice remarked. "That's nice. She needs to get out and meet some of the folks here. They seem to be a nice lot. A little fancy for my blood, but nice." She was putting away the dishes. Beatrice had always been happiest and most at ease puttering around the kitchen.

"I thought you might like to join us?" Timothy ventured. "It would be our pleasure to have you come along."

"Is that a fact now?" Beatrice was delighted. "Well, if it's your pleasure, it's my pleasure. A country fair in Lakeside, how about that! My Irving will be pleased that I'm invited. It's a pretty ritzy neighborhood my Rosalie lives in. I always knew she would do all right."

103

"Oh, yeah?" Rosalie was standing in the doorway dressed in a faded blue jeans outfit embroidered with colorful flowers and butterflies. She had a saucy broad-brimmed hat on her head and a pink scarf around her neck.

"Such a face!" Aunt Beatrice exclaimed, beaming.

"And the rest of her ain't bad either," Manuel put in.

Timothy's energy field malfunctioned only slightly. He was beginning to adjust, and reserved comment.

"We're going to a country fair," Aunt Beatrice announced, pleased and excited. "I haven't been to a fair since I left New Jersey. And here I am with a priest yet. Wait until Irving hears about this one."

"A fair?" Rosalie's eyes locked on Manuel. She tried to sound casual. "That's terrific. So they have fairs in heaven. I guess that's fair." She grinned and shrugged off her remark. "Not a good joke, but I tried."

She could not take her eyes away from Manuel's reciprocal gaze, and silently noted that he looked just as good in a shirt.

"There's a carnival, too," Manuel added. "A Ferris wheel and all the other carnival kind of jazz. The carousel is there all the time, but not the fair. The fair is a special occasion."

"Oh, yeah? Well, maybe I'll get lucky. Maybe they'll have a shooting gallery with crows for a target."

Timothy winced, another jolt for his energy field. Such thoughts were not indicative of growth. Her attitude was still in need of further alteration.

Manuel simply smiled.

"Who knows?" Aunt Beatrice replied with a grin. "Around here, anything is possible."

"God knows that's true," Manuel agreed.

"God knows," Timothy was forced to concede.

And they all left for the fair. ✳

Chapter Eleven

Starting near the far side of the lake, the fair extended into the surrounding countryside. The works of countless artists and craftsmen were exhibited, reflecting various levels of expertise in design in metal, wood, marble, clay, fabric, even plastic. There were many impressive paintings, posters, and tapestries created by souls who had been refining their artistry to near-perfection.

An eclectic assortment of animals and livestock from all over the world was on display, some familiar, others more or less a figment of the imagination. It was fascinating.

At the food exhibition, aspiring cooks and chefs from all over the world offered an amazing selection of delicate, aromatic, appetizing dishes for all to taste or feast upon. Everything was perfectly delicious. All things considered, Aunt Beatrice was a bit upset that she had not arrived prepared to enter at least one of the cooking competitions. But she did enjoy seeing all the fine needlepoint, knitting, and quilting—something she had always planned to get around to on earth with the very best of intentions.

The theatrical presentations by various actors, singers, and dancers were enjoyed by all. Many souls who had been famous at various times on earth now shared their talents and skills, teaching and guiding others in need of their sound judgment and expertise. William Shakespeare was an honored guest, though most souls there understood that he usually hung out at a much higher frequency. He had been invited to instruct a group of aspiring thespians and writers who had long hoped and prayed to meet him. They were delighted with his presence. The rendering of one of Shakespeare's sonnets by a young Celtic poet who in turn recited an uplifting ballad of his own was an inspiration for everyone present, and especially for Timothy.

Anything the mind of man could imagine and then some could be found at the fair. All the souls in that dimension had turned out in loving support. It was a way of measuring progress in terms of special talents and gifts that would enable souls to be of greater service in the Grand Design at some future time.

Many souls at that level were just beginning to learn that every earthly desire required some measure of fulfillment while on earth before a soul could advance to the next stage of growth and awareness. Each soul was at a different stage in that preparation.

And the carnival—it was grand. Gaiety, excitement, and laughter were everywhere. It was the way carnivals were designed to be, with barkers and belly dancers, snake charmers and strongmen, and even a bearded lady, which Rosalie found strange. And there was a Ferris wheel, a Tilt-a-Whirl, a Loop-the-Loop, and a Tunnel of Love. But no shooting galleries with crows for targets. In fact, there were no shooting galleries at all. But there were bumper cars and a house of mirrors, and the carousel. It was the largest, grandest, most magnificent carousel Rosalie had ever seen, with mythical beasts made of clear sparkling crystal: unicorns, winged lions, grand elephants with uplifted trunks, and Pegasus with wings held high. Each creature reflected prismatic beams of color as it circled round and round in shimmering, glimmering light. And the music was inspiring, beautiful—even sublime.

Time and time again Rosalie and Manuel rode around and around on the grand carousel. Rosalie sat upon the unicorn, and Manuel, the winged lion. As the glittering brass ring flashed by on each turn, Rosalie reached out to grab it. Yet no matter how hard she tried, each time the brass ring remained just out of reach.

"Someday," Manuel consoled her.

"But why not now? Today?" she protested, pouting.

"When you're ready, you'll catch it. Stop sulking. I'm not ready either."

"You're sounding awfully mysterious all of a sudden. What do you mean I'm not ready? You're not ready? What's to be ready?"

"You're just not. Take my word for it." He dismissed the matter with the tone of his voice and gazed deeply into her questioning eyes. "Okay?"

"Okay!" she relented, but tried one more time. She was grinning at him over her shoulder as the carousel slowed to a stop.

"I still wish I'd caught it. I've never caught a brass ring. It would have been terrific." It had been her first real disappointment in that dimension.

Manuel took her by the hand and gently pulled her in the direction of a hot dog vendor near the edge of the lake. Rosalie wondered how Aunt Beatrice and Timothy were doing at the food exhibits. Beatrice had been asked to help judge the baking contest, and Timothy was tasting the wines. There was talk that the local vineyards produced a heavenly bouquet.

"Spirits for the spirit," Timothy had quipped.

"Food for the soul," was Beatrice's happy response.

Little had changed. They seemed to be having a good time. Timothy could really loosen up for a priest. But then, Aunt Beatrice had a knack for making people enjoy life in any dimension.

"Do you know what I'd really like?" Rosalie remarked while finishing off her hot dog and nodding toward a cotton candy vendor near the lake.

"Gotcha!" Manuel replied. "Hot dogs and cotton candy! Coney Island in July! But the weather here is much nicer. Not all that muggy, if you'll pardon the pun."

They ate cotton candy while walking near the lake. People were out sailing, rowing, and paddling in canoes. A powerboat was towing a skier in its wake.

"Did you ever try that?" Rosalie asked, while watching the graceful skier glide through the water.

"Not me. I never had time or money for things like that."

"Me neither. But I don't think I would have liked it, anyway."

"Chicken?" he said with a knowing grin.

"Go to hell!" she retorted, but her eyes were smiling.

With mutual unspoken consent they sat down on the grass near where the water gently lapped against the shore. The sky was blue. The sun was shining. It was a perfect day for sitting beside a lake. The haunting music of the carousel serenaded them from the distance.

"How come you never got married?" she decided to ask.

"Nobody ever asked me," he winked in reply.

"Come on. Weren't you ever in love?"

"Yeah," he paused. "I guess I was in love once." His tone was somber as a curious look formed in his eyes. Then he continued, offhandedly, "I went to this whorehouse once, in Spanish Harlem. The girl was supposed to be Spanish, but it was hard to tell. She didn't speak Spanish, except maybe for 'si, si, senor.' She was a cute trick with a great body and a very pretty face. Not bad, all things considered. You see I'd never made it with a chick before. I was twenty-three, sexually retarded, and I wanted to find a hooker with a heart of gold. I'd seen a couple of movies, and I'd read this book that really turned me on about this guy who fell in love with a hooker, so I figured, why not me?"

He waited for her response. Rosalie just narrowed her eyes and studied him. She didn't say anything. She was waiting to hear the rest of his story.

"Her name was Marguerite," he finally said. "At least that's what she said her name was. And she had a heart of gold all right, four carats and metallic. She was nothing at all like the girl in the book or the movie. But it was an interesting experience. I learned a few things."

"Like what?" Her tone was sarcastic.

"Like don't waste fifty bucks on a Harlem whore when you can score in the Bronx for the price of popcorn and a movie. But Marguerite—I guess you could say she initiated me into the carnal rites of manhood. She turned a green, arrested adolescent into something of a veteran in just an hour and a half." He leaned back on the grass and watched Rosalie, an amused expression on his face.

"You call that being in love?" She shook her head in disgust. "That's pathetic, that's what that is."

"It wasn't so bad. I got my money's worth."

He sounded offhand, but somehow it didn't all feel right to her. For a moment she didn't know what to say. She just sat there, studying the quiet gentleness in his dark brown eyes and the strong characteristics in his finely chiseled face. She was sensing the soul of the man. The more she studied his face, the softer Manuel's expression became.

Then he spoke. "I was in love with an Irish girl from Queens once upon a time," he confessed, almost defensively. He guessed it might be best if he were honest with Rosalie, even though she was the nosiest girl he had ever met. Anyway, she would be reading his thoughts too soon enough. He knew it was only a matter of time.

"What was her name?" she asked, feeling relieved.

"Laura McKenzie." Now he was smiling and before she could ask he said, "She was a teacher for retarded kids." His eyes misted over. "Not that much to look at, really. She had one brown eye and one blue eye. I thought it was neat. She didn't have the greatest body. She was sort of flat-chested and bottom-heavy, but she sure did love those kids. What a heart that woman had, bigger than life. Laura taught me a lot about love." He stopped talking and stared at the lake a beat before adding, "She got leukemia and died."

"That's terrible!" Tears formed in Rosalie's eyes.

"At the time I thought it was absolutely unfair to take someone like Laura. I mean, she was only thirty. She had so much to give and was such a great person. She had inner strength and lots of character. She also knew how to die with dignity, real dignity. In that hospital ward filled with terminal patients nobody was a better trouper than Laura McKenzie—at least nobody I ever met. Laura was something else."

After a long moment Rosalie finally ventured, "Well, maybe she's here. You should ask around. Haven't you ever thought about finding her?"

"Sure, I tried. That's how I found out that she had gone on to bigger and better things."

The music of the carousel suddenly became louder, more intense. Its haunting refrain aroused a strange though familiar sensation in Rosalie. A soul memory stirred at the core of her being.

"Bigger and better things? What do you mean by that?" she finally asked.

"She's been recycled," he simply stated.

Rosalie was aghast, "You mean like plastic and glass?"

"It's heavenly ecology," Manuel informed her, a broad smile on his face. "Let's face it, it would be a waste of energy not to recycle it and put it to positive use. Right?"

"Sure," she was forced to agree after considerable hesitation, and was almost afraid to ask, "Exactly *what* has she gone on *to?*"

"She's been born again," he confessed, amused, then he quickly raised both hands in protest. "Don't ask me how or where or when. They don't give out that kind of information readily around here. They would only say she's a woman again—and this time both her eyes are blue. I know she's got to be happy on that score. It really bothered her having one of each color."

Rosalie's imagination had temporarily gone wild with the very idea of recycling. So Honey was right. People are born more than once. Energy has to be recycled. She shook her head in delight. Leave it to God to think up something like that!

So she decided to ask, "How come you were a virgin until you were twenty-three? I mean, you hear all these stories about Latinos being such red-hot lovers. What happened to you?"

"Well," Manuel began, bedazzled by her disarming ways, "You see, Mama always made a big deal about VD. You know—Virgin's Death. By the age of five she had me totally convinced that my penis would fall off if I touched it, let alone put it to constructive use. So I was over twenty before I found out that it works better if you use it, and it can't possibly fall off. Is there anything else at all that you'd like to know about my sex life as a Puerto Rican?"

"Not that I can think of right off," she countered, a sheepish grin on her face. "If there is, I'll let you know."

"I'm sure you will," he replied, and they both laughed.

Now they were looking at each other, really looking, with probing eyes. The way people do when they're not exactly sure what they're really looking for, or why they're even looking. It was chemistry. The Law of Gender: attraction in full measure. They were discovering that their energy fields were highly compatible. Each of them quickly became aware of a void that could only be filled by the other person's frequency. It was a special moment—a time of awakening.

Rosalie had that sensation of butterflies fluttering in the pit of her stomach—a warm, wonderful, extraordinary sensation. As for Manuel, he felt helpless. Women could do that to him sometimes. Women he found attractive. Women like Rosalie. He had found Laura McKenzie attractive. There had been something familiar, something special about her. But his feeling for Rosalie was more, much more. It was a comfortable, warm melting that started at his core and filled him up—a feeling he thought could last for a very long time, maybe forever. Each of them was learning—learning about love. Love that comes in many sizes and shapes, many colors and hues. Manuel was learning all about love. So was Rosalie.

All at once Rosalie's attention was magnetically drawn toward a couple strolling near the edge of the lake—a tall, handsome man with dark hair and a mustache and a beautiful, blonde woman. Rosalie stared in utter astonishment. Could it be him? He looked just like him. At least the way he looked in his old movies on television. And the woman Rosalie had only seen in very old movies. Never in a theater, like she had his movies. But the woman sure did look like her.

Rosalie got a strange tingly sensation. Her energy field increased its frequency. Her heart center was vibrating at a rapid rate. "I think I'm having hallucinations," she finally admitted in a whisper, drawing Manuel's attention to the couple walking toward them. "Do you see who I see or am I just freaking out or something?" She couldn't take her eyes off the man and woman as they walked even closer.

Manuel studied them, then informed her, "It seems to me that I'm seeing what you're seeing, unless we're having the same hallucination."

"Rhett Butler," her voice was just above a whisper. "Now I know I'm in heaven."

Rosalie's energy field expanded and contracted in subtle, multicolored streams of ecstasy as Clark Gable and Carole Lombard walked by them, hand in hand.

"I saw *Gone with the Wind* seven times," she declared like a moonstruck teenager. "I fell in love with him when I was seven."

"I only saw it four times," Manuel admitted. "And I never was crazy about that Scarlett O'Hara. That kind of woman is bad news. Now Miss Melanie, she was a good woman."

"Scarlett deserved to lose him," Rosalie admitted, a look of anguish on her face as she watched the man of her dreams walk by with the lady who had played such an important role in his life.

Gable turned to smile his memorable smile, nodding his appreciation to Rosalie for her unabashed admiration. Face it, whatever the dimension, a star was a star was a star. And Gable looked young and vibrant, so alive. Rosalie was really beginning to enjoy some of the distinct advantages of being dead.

"I can't believe that I really saw them here in Lakeside. Imagine!"

"I saw Harlow once," Manual admitted, a soft smile on his face.

"Jean Harlow?" Rosalie was still in a semi-swoon over Gable, though by now he and Carole Lombard had disappeared into the crowd.

Suddenly she wondered why she hadn't thought of something intelligent to say to him? Why hadn't she reached out and tried to touch him? His smile had really said it all. He knew it was Rhett Butler that she loved. The romantic, dashing, lovable rogue—Rhett.

For a brief moment, Rosalie could see Rhett and Scarlett at Twelve Oaks in the library—and in Atlanta inside their grand mansion, standing on the long, winding staircase together. And near the end of the movie at the front door.

"Frankly, Scarlett," Manuel affected, "I don't give a damn."

"Wasn't it awful?" Tears flowed down Rosalie's cheeks. She cried every time she saw the movie. "She waited too long to find out that she really needed him. She was selfish, but he loved her. He would have given her everything, but she was just too wrapped up in her selfish little self." Rosalie was weeping.

"Come on," Manuel consoled, putting an arm around her. "It was just a movie, a story, that's all."

"It was more than a movie," Rosalie was sobbing her heart out. "It was life. Life can be like that. People can discover too late that they've lost something they should have appreciated and held onto. It happens all the time. People can just get too wrapped up in themselves. Why are people so blind? Why?"

"You know something," he teased. "You can really get carried away."

"You don't have a romantic bone in your body," she proclaimed, pushing him away.

"Sure, I do. In fact, I'm so romantic that I'm going to take you for a ride in the Tunnel of Love. I may not be Rhett Butler, but you have yet to see Manuel Sierra in action. Who knows? You may find out that I'm a combination of Clark Gable, Errol Flynn, and Douglas Fairbanks, Jr.! I really used to like his movies." Affecting an English accent, "He was a bit of all right with that sword of his."

Manuel leaped to his feet to assume a swashbuckling pose. "I am prepared to defend your honor, O' Damsel of the Unicorn. I am a defender of the faith," he proclaimed, fencing an imaginary opponent. "Oh, no, you don't, Black Knight. This lady is mine."

In an instant Manuel became fully clothed in Spanish armor and was fencing with a Moor, swords crossed to the hilt. Rosalie could hear the clash of metal. The eyes of the Moor were filled with terror. He began backing away, retreating under Manuel's fearless gaze. Then as suddenly as he had appeared, he was gone. Manuel's armor dissolved back into his patchwork shirt and blue jeans.

"What was that?" Rosalie was rubbing her eyes and squinting at the now sword-less Manuel.

"A memory, I guess." Manuel's eyes misted over. "You saw him, too, huh?" He helped Rosalie to her feet.

"What do you mean, a memory?" She was searching the area to see where the Moor had gone. He was nowhere in sight.

"I've been having these insights lately—about being a Spanish soldier when the Moors invaded Spain. I mean, I was one hell of a swashbuckler. And every time I say *Douglas Fairbanks, Jr.,* this guy appears. I get the feeling that he was the last person I saw in that lifetime. I also get the feeling that I buckled when I should have swashed—if you get the picture."

"Jesus!" was her only response.

"That's probably what I said," he remarked with a grin. "I was a good Catholic, no doubt, or else why would I have fought the infidel who thought he was fighting the infidel?" He shook his head and shrugged. "Evidently, I got the point, so to speak, and in his mind I accepted the faith. They called them holy wars, when there's nothing the least bit holy about war. How long do you suppose it will take humanity to figure that one out?"

"Who knows? I hope before it's too late." For a Puerto Rican from the Bronx he was turning out to be quite sensitive and sensible.

"For a Jewish chick from Brooklyn you're not so bad yourself," was his quick reply.

"That isn't fair," Rosalie complained. Why should he be able to read her mind when she could not yet read his?

"It's not that I'm anti-Semitic, just anti-female. It's a hang-up from my past life that keeps hanging on."

"Is that fair?" she asked.

"Learning is fair and growing is fair."

"I thought God was supposed to be fair."

"The fair's fair," he said, taking her hand. "Come on, sexy, I'll get you another hot dog and take you for a ride in the Tunnel of Love. You'll like it. I promise," and with that he began dragging her along beside him.

"Do you really think I'm sexy?" she was trying to sound casual as she stumbled along.

"Of course, I think you're sexy." He didn't look at her when he said it, but when they reached the hot dog stand he turned to her with a serious expression on his face. "Do you think you could have been Spanish once? I mean, no one but me has ever seen that guy before. Maybe you were there. Maybe you were with me."

"You probably died in my arms," she replied offhandedly, but a cold shiver ran all the way through her.

"Nice," he replied. "So what about you? They raped the women and made them slaves."

"I don't know," she replied as another shiver rippled through her. "If something like that happened, I'd just as soon forget, wouldn't you?"

"Yeah," he admitted, handing her a hot dog with ketchup and mustard, just the way she liked it. "Some people may be better off not remembering, but someday we'll have to remember. We have to come to the point where we understand why it all happened. How we created it all. It's the only way we can get beyond it all eventually."

"I guess that's logical," she conceded, but for the moment she didn't really want to learn so fast. "I'll think about it tomorrow." A sly smile played upon her lips.

"Like Scarlett O'Hara?"

"No, more like Rosalie Rosenberg," she said, batting her eyes as she took a bite of hot dog. Then she looked him right in the eye and asked point-blank, "So where's the Tunnel of Love?"

Chapter Twelve

From all outward appearances, the Tunnel of Love was just that, similar to those found at amusement parks on earth, yet far grander. Not the least bit tacky. The entrance was designed like a large open heart, edged in a gathering of exquisite white lace. Large white marble cupids were poised on either side, holding great golden bows and arrows aimed at the center of the heart. From the points of the arrows streamed brilliant beams of golden-white light that diffused at the entrance of the tunnel, casting a misty glow.

Large baskets of roses—red, pink, yellow, peach, and white—were placed in just the right spots, their sweet fragrance filling the air. The scene was something straight out of a romance novel. A childhood storybook. A fairy tale. It was perfect.

Rosalie and Manuel stepped into a small boat shaped like a large white swan. Inside were deep, soft, pink velvet cushions with antique lace around the edges. Once they were comfortably seated, the boat slowly began to glide through the great open heart into a long, dimly lit tunnel.

They were sailing through misty, diffused light along a passageway. Once well inside the tunnel, the light disappeared and everything became pitch-dark. Yet shortly, a faint rosy glow enveloped them, and sweet, angelic music began to soothe their very souls.

Rosalie and Manuel were being carried on a pink cloud, drifting through infinite space serenaded by the music of the spheres. Countless twinkling stars filled the vastness all around them. It was really quite special. It was then they first sensed the love waves. Blissful, glorious, ecstatic waves of love that vibrated from the core of their being outward to totally fill and surround them—the true essence of Love.

Manuel took Rosalie's hand in his, and in an instant, the two hands became as one. It was strange yet natural. The blending of their vital forces endowed each of them with a greater sense of purpose, a sense of true and lasting destiny. They were caught up as in a dream yet not altogether dreaming. The core of their being was now united in purpose and love more profound than that experienced by most ordinary mortals. It was love transcendent. They were now in absolute union, fully aware that that unity belonged to all creatures and all beings. It was Life in its pristine essence, unity far beyond the biological urge to mate. And yet, at a lower frequency it was that same impulse that served the Source in providing physical vehicles for souls in need of further experience upon the earth. Experience that served the fulfillment of the Divine Evolutionary Plan. It was something rather grand.

They were separate yet one, part of the ebb and flow of Creation, briefly centered, removed from the wheel of eternal motion and exalted above the elements. They were being blessed, truly blessed—relieved of the pain and suffering of mortality and bathed in eternal Love. Love that heals. They were renewing their souls. In their sincere seeking they had become that which they so earnestly sought: beginningless, endless Love.

Through unspoken mutual consent the link uniting their hearts and souls had been strengthened. Their souls were now united in purpose to become totally that which each had only been in part. By seeking love in one another they had found the Source of love deep within.

They continued to drift as in a dream, vibrating, musical waves of color all around them. Red. Orange. Yellow. Green. Blue. Pink. Purple. Violet. Geometrical designs—circles, squares, triangles, hexagons, octagons. Stars—five-pointed, six-pointed, seven-pointed, eight. Beautiful, floating, abstract designs. Rosalie and Manuel were high on Spirit. The experience was internal and external at the same time. It was truly something else.

Rosalie's left hand rested in Manuel's right, sweetly touching. Orgasm had been nothing like this—simply a promise of more to come. In their kiss ecstasy was complete, total perfection—a kiss to seal a promise. Their souls would continue to strive for love transcendent. When they left the tunnel they would not consciously remember, but the imprint would indelibly remain in their souls. The imprint would guide them toward ultimate perfection. Time would plot their course. Reaching the goal could well take lifetimes, but success was assured. It was simply a matter of being alive, alive in any dimension.

A deep, profound, dream-filled sleep carried them back through time. Their souls were remembering, reviewing other sometimes fragmentary realities that appeared like threads in a giant tapestry being woven by the Infinite. The Tunnel of Love became a Tunnel of Time, taking them back, back, back into the remote past, into ages recorded in the annals of history, in the memory of nature. They were unraveling the scrolls of time that exist within the ethers of eternity.

Unfurling before their minds' eye was the pageantry and splendor of ancient Egypt during the reign of Ramses II. Land of the Pharaohs. Land of the pyramids. Each of them had been a slave in the royal household that ruled in pomp and glory in that ancient Egyptian land. Manuel re-experienced his role as an oarsman on the royal barge that sailed the Nile, Rosalie her role as a servant laboring in the royal kitchens. Their love had bloomed in stolen moments of ecstasy beneath the shadow of the great Sphinx. It had been a life of fear and futile frustration. A life of enslavement to a will not their own. It was then their souls first met on the earth plane a very, very long time ago.

Three hundred years later their paths crossed again in another royal household in the grand and elegant palace of King Solomon. Once more Rosalie was a servant girl. This time she attended to the considerable and controversial harem of the king. No easy task. She had hoped to make concubine, but as fate would have it, she never made the grade. Face it, she was no raving beauty that time around. And she knew in her heart that good old King Solomon had neither the time nor the energy for even one more concubine. He barely got around to enjoying the ones he already had. After all, his three hundred wives kept him busy whenever they got lucky and their number came up. Solomon did always try to be fair in such matters.

In most respects, life in Solomon's harem was more interesting and educational than slaving in Ramses' kitchen, although both courts provided an earful when it came to pithy gossip. Manuel was one of the eunuchs who guarded Solomon's harem. This was where his serious hang-ups regarding women actually began, understandably. Nevertheless, he and Rosalie did become good friends, which was all they could manage under the circumstances. It was sympathy, another facet of love that fortified the bond between them.

In Macedonia, six centuries later they were born into the same family as brothers. Manuel was the eldest by three years. During their youth they became fine athletes, and then strong and skillful soldiers in their manhood. Their fates became linked with Alexander the Great on his campaigns and conquests into the arid land of Egypt, which seemed somehow familiar at the time. During a surprise attack, however, both of them were killed in battle and buried near the tomb of the leader they had served and loved. In Egypt they died free men, not slaves, which was a distinct improvement from an evolutionary perspective.

Another six hundred years passed before their souls met again on the earth. Near Rome in the third century A.D., they were born as man and woman to different parents. They met during their adolescence. It was love at first sight. They were married young and raised a large family of eight children.

Early in that life Manuel tilled the land. Rosalie kept the house and family garden. Their sons and daughters were taught to care for the geese, cows, mules, sheep and goats. They enjoyed a simple farm life. It was in Rome that Manuel first took a serious interest in architecture, though he lacked the opportunity to educate himself in such matters. He was constantly amazed by the wonders erected in the modern Rome of his time. In stolen moments he sketched and secretly planned his future home. By a strange turn of fate he was taught how to grow grapes. His vineyards provided fine wine for the noblemen's tables. There on the outskirts of Rome their lives were long and full and rich. Manuel died just a year after Rosalie. The children buried them side by side on a hill overlooking the vineyards they had come to treasure.

Four centuries later they showed up in Afghanistan. Rosalie became a camel driver and profited from raising camels. Manuel became his favorite and youngest wife. Their roles were reversed. Jealousies arose amongst the wives. The oldest one nearly succeeded in poisoning poor Manuel. After that things were never quite the same. His resentment toward women at the soul level deepened—an unfortunate twist of fate. Members of a nomadic tribe, they roamed the desert living in tents. They spent that lifetime wandering from oasis to oasis.

In Spain they were married yet again. Manuel was a soldier anxious to defend his country against the invading Moors. He eventually did get the point, so to speak. Straight through, as fate would have it. He left his young, devoted, pregnant wife alone with two small sons. Two months later she died giving birth to a daughter, thereby escaping the terrors of the time. It was not one of their happier lives. Their three orphaned children were raised by dispassionate relatives, yet they grew to live productive lives in their times.

The very next century their paths crossed in Persia. The uncle who raised Manuel was one of the architects who were busy renovating the royal palace. Manuel's interest in architecture was sparked once more, yet proved insufficient for much advancement that time around. Instead, he took an easy way out and became a merchant peddling fabrics, baubles, bangles and beads throughout the countryside.

Rosalie finally made concubine that time around, fulfilling the yearning that had started back in Solomon's harem. She belly danced before the sultan and his cronies. She was quite good, all things considered. Genghis Khan periodically marauded through the province with his Mongol warriors, terrorizing the countryside, adding spice to their existence. On occasion Rosalie plied Manuel with her womanly wiles, primarily to finagle baubles, bangles, and bits of brocade and silk. They fooled around but never married during that lifetime. Manuel was especially fond of Persia.

Just less than a hundred years later Rosalie was a servant once again. She was obviously having some trouble with her self-image. This time it was China, the Court of Kublai Khan at Kaifeng. Marco Polo was a favorite at court. Manuel made Captain of the Royal Guard—not bad from his perspective. They were working on separate karma that lifetime, so they barely met. Court life in China was stuffy and formal, not at all conducive to hanky-panky like it had been back in Persia.

In their journey through the ages Rosalie briefly reexamined her life as a young boy in the Italian countryside. Mid-fourteenth century. The boy took great pleasure in shooting one bird after another with a slingshot for the sheer sport of killing. An aging scarecrow filled with straw stood in a nearby field with a black crow perched on its outstretched arm. It was elementary information for the soul, a poignant reminder.

In Romania, Manuel and Rosalie were again wed. It was the early sixteen hundreds. Members of a band of wandering gypsies during the reign of Michael the Brave, they were born in Transylvania. Once more their roles were reversed. Rosalie was a cheat, a horse thief, a scoundrel, and a consummate ladies' man. Manuel was a beauty. He sang and danced. He had long, black hair, big black eyes, and a voluptuous figure.

The soul of Honey MacIntosh was Rosalie's elder sister in the small gypsy band. She read tea leaves and Tarot cards in the hamlets and villages, earning her living by telling fortunes for the rich. Basically an honest woman, she earnestly tried to persuade her younger brother to abandon his life of thievery and crime, all to no avail.

Manuel, by most standards, was a vixen, taunting and flaunting. A ravishing beauty he was. Rosalie was often jealous with good cause, though she, too, played at infidelity. It was tit for tat. David was also there in the gypsy camp. As Rosalie's uncle, he played a paternal role, trying to set young Rosalie straight. Yet she was a hard-headed man with a mind of her own. As fate would have it, she was eventually hanged for stealing horses—quick karma that time around.

During their French incarnations, Rosalie became a lady-in-waiting to Marie Antoinette, serving once again, but this time in the French court as a member of the aristocracy. She was a coquettish and poised beauty. It was a necessary check in her evolutionary process to balance out the aggressive male tendencies manifested in Romania.

Manuel was a French nobleman who frequented the court. He was married to another woman when he met Rosalie, but they became lovers. They were much better behaved than in Romania, though there was considerable gossip at court. Once the revolution was in full swing their romance was cut short. In more ways than one you could say they lost their heads.

Roughly fifty years later they met yet again. Born to beg in the streets of London, Rosalie turned to the world's oldest profession. She became a young prostitute. Her heart wasn't really in it, but she did manage to sustain herself.

Manuel was born out of wedlock to a Welsh peasant girl who had succumbed to the passions of a French sailor in port. Through a bit of good karma he was apprenticed to a stonemason. His specialty was tombstones. Most souls didn't live too long at the time, so his work kept him busy.

It was on his first trip to London that he met young Rosalie in the streets. One look and he took the young girl to his heart, saving her from a life in the gutter. Actually, he owed it to her after his shenanigans in France. So little did Manuel realize when back in the Bronx that the hooker with a heart of gold he was looking for was really Rosalie. A few years after they married they migrated to America with two young sons in hand. Crossing the Atlantic proved extremely difficult. Their younger son died from dysentery and was buried at sea. But in the New World three more children were destined to be born into their family.

Manuel's success as a stonemason was assured in America. There was a full-scale civil war in progress. Tombstones were much needed. Thousands of men, young and old, were sacrificing their lives to reunite a nation divided and torn with strife. In late 1863 they moved into a modest clapboard house near Gettysburg, thereby becoming citizens in a new nation, a nation throwing off the bonds of slavery. A nation founded on an ideal dedicated to preserving freedom and human rights for all people regardless of race, color, or creed.

Rosalie and Manuel's excursion through the Tunnel of Love had been like being in an epic movie with each of them playing many parts. It was their souls that had reviewed lifetimes that were shared, not their mortal minds. From that moment on, each of them would be forced to grope in the dark until their souls reached a full measure of Light, a full measure of understanding. There had been many life-times when they had lived separately and apart. It was their shared lives that were important to them now—personal history lessons with chapters yet to be written in the Book of Life.

Once more Rosalie and Manuel drifted in total darkness, peaceful beyond description. Slowly, the two of them began to awaken from the dream of their souls. Forgotten moments shared once again were to become forgotten. Faint stars twinkled all around them, eventually becoming giant, bright, shining stars.

When Rosalie looked at Manuel, his eyes sparkled like two radiant stars, resplendently shining. For Manuel, Rosalie's entire being was a bright shining star of love.

"Twinkle, twinkle, little star," Manuel whispered, holding her closely.

Rosalie didn't answer. She was at peace, filled with certain joy.

As the boat slowly drifted out of the tunnel the bright light of the sun surrounded them. Their hands were touching without grasping. Atoms in affinity remain in close proximity. There was no need to grasp. Their souls were of one accord. Each of them had grown in love and understanding.

In shining splendor before them was the beautiful carousel. The crystal unicorn and Pegasus were reflecting all the colors of the rainbow in an enormous prism of light. Garlands of roses encircled the necks of the majestic, mythical beasts as the haunting music of the carousel played in melodious strains. Rosalie caught a glimpse of the brass ring, shining in the sunlight, reflecting beams of the One Sun glowing in the heavens above.

One day you won't escape me, she thought. One day I'll catch you and keep you. When I'm ready, but not just yet.

Manuel too saw the brass ring sparkling in the light. He had read her thoughts and understood, somehow knowing full well that he would be the first one to catch the brass ring. For a brief moment that realization saddened his heart, and he tightened his grip on Rosalie's small hand as the music of the carousel played on. ✳

Chapter Thirteen

The fair was a tremendous success. Aunt Beatrice went back to Seaside knowing she had helped choose the finest chocolate cake ever baked. It was absolute perfection. Timothy had enjoyed himself immensely, for the wine makers had outdone themselves. And Rosalie and Manuel were in love.

Manuel could now return to his remote mountaintop with the consolation that there was someone special with whom to share eternity. He would now endeavor to create structures more magnificent than the Taj Mahal in tribute to his love. He would write glorious verses extolling his love. He would become a great architect of divine designs, with Rosalie as his inspiration. His heart was certainly vibrating at a fabulous frequency.

Rosalie agreed to visit Aunt Beatrice in Seaside sometime soon. Tomorrow she would go to Manuel's mountain. She would see paradise from his perspective. Tomorrow their love would blossom and grow.

Timothy lingered in the den, enjoying his usual biscuits and tea. Rosalie and Manuel lingered in the moonlight, taking their sweet time saying good-bye. To Timothy's way of thinking it seemed like forever; although he understood from his past experiences on earth that it could be that way with young love. Here he surmised love was always young whenever love was renewed. It was eternal love that seemed such a rarity among couples Timothy had met. Love beyond mortal blindness. The kind of love unconditionally expressed by Marcella and Matthias. Timothy longed to express that kind of love one day, though he had learned that it involved a vibratory frequency located deep within, yet all around—a frequency that had to be cultivated and earned.

From the far side of the lake one could hear the faint, melodious music of the carousel. It was not unlike a tune that plays over and over in the mind, the music of dreams, haunting yet sublime.

Timothy patiently waited, sipping his tea, as a parent awaits the return of a child. For Rosalie was in his charge. They had business in need of further attention.

"Oh, Timothy," she sighed from the open doorway, her expression dreamy. "Isn't he the most wonderful man in the whole world? The most wonderful human being you have ever met?"

"You could say that," Timothy concurred, an understanding smile on his lips. "That is, surely now, he must be."

Rosalie walked over to her favorite recliner, unconsciously swaying to the faint music of the carousel.

Nothing like a good dose of love waves to make the heart receptive, Timothy thought to himself.

"I'm going to his mountaintop," she announced, misty-eyed, then sat down. "We're going to walk in the forest and talk to nature spirits. Manuel says he knows nature spirits personally, and Timothy, I believe him."

"That he does, lass. I taught him to converse with them myself," Timothy explained. "Let's face it, there's nothing like an Irishman to put you in touch with the wee folk. No, sirree! Some of my best friends are fairies."

"I met a few fairies in California but I wouldn't call them nature spirits," she replied in an attempt at humor that was lost on Timothy.

"Is that a fact now?" he responded in interest. "I must visit the place one day and see for myself. But then, nature spirits are everywhere, lass."

As Rosalie pushed back in the recliner, the television screen filled with light. Then it filled with David's face. He looked sad and forlorn, dejected and alone. There were tears in his eyes.

"Oh, my God!" Rosalie caught her breath. Her mind began racing. Here she was in another dimension taking rides through the Tunnel of Love with Manuel, ready to run off to his mountaintop retreat, and there poor David was on earth, all alone and stricken with grief.

"Here I am, barely dead, having a great time, and there he is with nobody while I've already got somebody. Talk about fickle, ye gods!"

She was overcome with guilt at how quickly she could feel love for someone else. Her adolescent behavior was brought to an abrupt halt. Everything was taking on a new perspective now. Of course, her feelings for David had never overwhelmed her to the extent that her feelings for Manuel did. All she had to do was look at Manuel to feel like a helpless sixteen-year-old who had never experienced an infatuation before, except maybe for Rhett Butler.

When she first met David she thought he was cute. His bringing back the money had certainly said something about his character. David had been good to her. There had been good times, wonderful times. But what she felt for Manuel was special, really special. Something she could not begin to describe. When she was around him there was this enormous magnetic pull, a sensation that went beyond time and space. It was unexplainable, something different from anything she had ever felt with David.

And yet, David loved her, even after living with her for four years. He had endured her nagging and bitching, her terrible complaining, and still he loved her. And now, there he was in North Hollywood with nobody, while here she was in Lakeside with somebody. Somehow, it didn't seem fair. And the worst part of it was, she didn't miss him—not one bit. She was having too much fun making so many wonderful discoveries about living in another dimension. No question about it, she was faced with a problem of monumental proportions.

"Concentrate, lass," Timothy gently admonished. "Send David loving thoughts of comfort and hope. Let him know you're all right. Let him know you don't blame him. He has a life to live, Rosalie. He's young. Let him know that you want him to live his life, that you want him to get on with it."

She stared at Timothy a long moment. He had to be right. There had to be a way to let David know, the same as there had been with Papa. The same as Aunt Beatrice's talks with Uncle Irving. She turned to the television and watched David closely. She was determined to try.

"I'm okay, David," she spoke just above a whisper, remorse in her voice. Naturally, she was feeling guilty. How was she supposed to tell her husband about another man when she was supposed to be dead and wasn't dead at all? It would have to be a bummer for him, regardless of how she told him. So she took a deep breath and let it out slowly.

"You see, David," she started, then stopped cold. Now he was crying, rubbing his forehead with his fingers and sobbing his heart out. He knows, she decided. He has to know. Not only do I die, I jilt him. The thoughts were racing through her mind. Guilt, guilt, guilt! She began to cry, too.

"For Chrissake, David, stop already. I'm sorry!" She was blowing her nose. "How was I to know they'd have such great guys over here? Let's face it, David, I'm no good. Maybe I was never unfaithful to you on earth because I never had the opportunity. Who knows? To tell you the absolute truth, I don't know what I would have done if I'd met Manuel there in North Hollywood or maybe Encino. Think of it as a blessing, David. Thank God I didn't meet him there. I could have turned into a regular Scarlett O'Hara. Who the hell knows, David? Who the hell knows?"

Timothy patiently allowed her to work through it, though her approach was not what he had in mind. "You are no longer married to David, Rosalie," he gently informed her, praying that the knowledge would change her vibratory frequency.

"But," she protested, continuing to sniffle. She had really been getting into her misery, unconsciously keeping up the momentum.

"Till death do you part, remember?" Timothy reminded her. "You were only married until death, Rosalie. When you fell off that roof your marriage was dissolved on the spot. You are a free woman. You are no longer married to David."

Rosalie regained self-control, then smiled and asked, "You mean it was sort of like instant divorce?"

"Less sticky, I'd say."

"So why am I sitting here feeling so miserable?" she asked, turning to look at David. Now he was blowing his nose, wiping away the tears.

"Did you hear that, David? It's all over between us—just like that!" She snapped her fingers. "I feel badly about it, David, really I do. But let's face it, I didn't plan on leaving so soon. I thought maybe I'd stick around another thirty–forty years, but my time was up, David. It was as simple as that."

She sat forward and spoke in loving tones, "And you have a life, David. A life to live. Really. You're young. You're only thirty, for Chrissake, so live! Go ahead and live, you deserve it." She was feeling better, at least.

Then David began beating his forehead with his fist. More tears rolled down his face.

"David, come on," she cried out, "let up, already. What in the hell can I do? I mean, I'm here and you're there. I want to help you David, but you're a stubborn man just like Uncle Irving, who keeps watering the lilies. You just don't listen!"

She began to find a quiet center within her being, then spoke to him from there. "You want to know something, David? I saw Aunt Beatrice. You never knew her. I used to tell you about her. I used to talk about her a lot. She's here,

David, and does she look terrific! And you want to know something else? She and Uncle Irving communicate. They talk. So I thought maybe I could communicate with you. I'm trying, David, really trying. I'm trying very hard to let you know that I'm fine. Just fine."

Rosalie got up from the chair and went to the television in an effort to get closer to David.

"So I've found somebody else," she confessed. "It was quick, I'll admit it. But big deal! You want I should be alone for the rest of eternity? It's not practical, David. And it would be lonely. Really lonely. Go find yourself a nice, Jewish girl. Get married, already. Raise a family the way you always wanted to, David. Don't just sit around blubbering because I died. It's not going to make you feel any better."

"Feel better, David, a lot better. Find yourself someone who will help take care of you. You need someone, David, someone to read your chapters to. A girl who can tell you that you're wonderful. Every man needs that, David. And do you need it! Believe me, I know. You're insecure and you shouldn't be because you're a great guy, David. And keep on writing your book until it's done. Who knows, someday you could be a rich man like you always hoped and dreamed and wanted to be. Then everyone will listen to what you have to say. Please finish the book, David. I'll go crazy if I never find out how it ends. You never told me. Do you realize that? How do you think that makes me feel? I mean, do I have to keep on wondering forever?"

David was beginning to look better, less distressed. He had stopped crying. He had stopped beating his forehead with his fist. His spirits had lifted. He got up from where he had been sitting with Rosalie's cigar box filled with mementos, her scrapbook of yesterdays, and he approached the desk to wistfully glance down at the unfinished manuscript. He had barely started the eighteenth chapter.

The story was about an innocuous bookkeeper who had absconded with over a million dollars of his company's funds. In the last chapter the bookkeeper had been trying to decide what to do with the money. Serious crooks from the Mafia were woven into the plot. David had never actually decided how to end the story. He stared at the manuscript, narrowing his eyes. Maybe writing would help take his mind off Rosalie. Maybe it would help him get a better grip. It was worth a try.

"Thatta boy, David!" Rosalie cheered, jumping up and down, tears in her eyes. "I know you can do it. Give it hell, David. And give my love to Morris."

"Morris?" Timothy inquired.

"Morris is the bookkeeper," Rosalie explained. "The guy who embezzled the money from this chemical company who deals in germ warfare." Rosalie went over to Timothy.

"You see, Morris feels justified in stealing the money because nobody ever thought he was important. Nobody noticed him or even bothered to talk to him, not even to say 'Good morning, Morris. How are you today?' So he embezzled the money from this company that was inventing these terrible germs to fight the enemy. They planned to kill people off with horrible diseases, with germs that can cripple bodies and brains, germs that are terrible beyond belief. Let's face it, Timothy, germ warfare has to be the worse possible answer to solving people's problems there on earth. Suppose you just gave the world the common cold? That would be bad enough, but crippling diseases? That's inhuman and savage."

"So naturally, Morris feels justified in stealing the money. Then the scientists will have less money to experiment with, and it will take them that much longer to find ways to kill people off with germs. I mean, why don't the goddamn chemists try to cure all the ills in the world? Doesn't that make more sense? No, instead they go and dream up atomic bombs that kill millions of people in one explosion. What in hell is the matter with the scientists? Are they all lunatics? Are they all just plain crazy?"

"We're all trying to help the world, lass," Timothy assured her. "Truly we are."

"Well, you all had better try harder and faster, before the germ scientists wipe out the entire population with their nasty concoctions." She had really gotten into the spirit of David's book.

"You tell them, David!" she cried out, fired with enthusiasm. "Tell them how to save the world from the maniacs. You can do it, David. I know you can."

David picked up a blank piece of paper and inserted it into the typewriter. For a long moment he stared at the blank page. Nothing was happening. Then he scowled, purpose and intent in his eyes, and all at once he began to type. He felt inspired. After all, his story dealt with issues the world needed to consider. People needed to know what he had to say. People needed to think about the consequences of imprudent, merciless acts against the human race.

"Hooray!" Rosalie cheered, jumping up and down in the middle of the room. "David Rosenberg is going to tell that world how to shape up. You just wait and see, Timothy O'Toole. He'll give those germ warfare geniuses what for." She ran to the television screen. "Do it, David. Do it! And will you please let me know how it ends."

She plopped down on the floor in front of the television screen and sat cross-legged, watching David. She was delighted that he was working.

The image of David on the screen suddenly picked up in momentum. He was typing, typing, typing; faster, faster, and faster. Rosalie watched him, convinced of her importance in inspiring his work. Then the picture again slowed to normal and the angle widened as a girl walked into the room from the kitchen. She was carrying a tray. On a plate was a sandwich with pickles and potato chips. There was a glass filled with ice and cola. Rosalie sat bolt upright, taken aback.

"That was fast. One minute I tell him to find himself a girl. The next thing I know, he has. That's gratitude for you."

"The lass looks somewhat familiar," Timothy cautiously ventured.

Rosalie narrowed her eyes, staring at the girl, whose face now filled the television screen. She could hardly believe her eyes. It was Honey MacIntosh. But she looked different. And she was smiling, really smiling, as she was serving David his lunch.

"Now just a minute!" Rosalie jumped to her feet, and began pacing. "Why in hell does she look so good?" She stared at Honey, trying to figure it out. That was when Honey handed David his sandwich and kissed him on the cheek.

"That's for inspiration," Honey cooed.

David coyly smiled. That did it!

"You bitch!" Rosalie exclaimed. "The minute I die and turn my back, you move in on my husband. Of all the lousy tricks, this one has got to be the worst." Rosalie's energy field was flashing bright red.

Timothy centered himself in white light to escape the chaotic vibrations filling the room. For a moment, his energy field felt as though it had been struck full force by a tornado.

"Who in the hell do you think you are, anyway?" Rosalie was yelling at Honey. "I'm supposed to be your best friend, remember? The one you should have warned not to climb up on roofs!"

Honey sat down opposite David, watching him eat his sandwich. Her eyes were the eyes of a woman in love as David started reading from the chapter he had just finished between mouthfuls of corned beef and rye. He was involved in the story and the sandwich. David loved corned beef. His second favorite was pastrami.

Honey looked quite different. She had lost weight and her strawberry blonde hair that usually straggled all over the place had been cut off just above her chin. It looked cute. And Honey was wearing makeup. She had taken a course at modeling school, and now she was totally revamped. She had always worn oversized clothing to hide her chubby body.

She was no longer chubby. Her clothes fit, and she had a nice figure. No wonder Honey was bringing David his sandwich with kosher dills, Rosalie thought. Honey had been around throughout their entire courtship. She knew everything David liked and everything David didn't like. Honey had given Rosalie advice about how to snag him. Honey read a lot. Until Rosalie died she had never had the chance to take advantage of the information. She was always a mess. Now she looked terrific, really terrific.

Rosalie never realized that Honey could look this good, or else she never would have told her all those things about David. Like how he likes his feet massaged after he writes because of the tension in his toes. For at that very moment, right in front of her eyes, Honey MacIntosh was taking off David's shoes to massage his toes. If that wasn't intimacy, what was?

"How did this happen so fast?" Rosalie was dismayed. "I only died a couple of days ago. I mean, I'm not even cold in my grave yet."

"Remember when we talked about time?" he reminded her. "It isn't the same here as it is on earth."

"Sure, tell me another story. A funny one."

"It's all rather relative and difficult to explain."

"So how long has it been?" she asked, keeping a close watch on Honey's foot massage. David was thoroughly enjoying himself. What had happened to his grief? His tears? The cigar box? The scrapbook? "How can you do this to me, David? She's a goy. When your mother gets wind of this is she ever going to raise hell—her son with a shiksa! She'll have a heart attack and die, David."

She began yelling at him, "She's a Gentile, David, a tea leaf-reading Gentile. Think of your mother. She'll blame you. She'll disown you." She stopped a moment, thoughtful. "So what's to disown, a gold watch maybe? A half-carat diamond? They've never been rich, the Rosenbergs."

"Nearly a year has passed on earth," Timothy informed her.

"You've got to be kidding," Rosalie was amazed. "How can it be a whole year? It seems like I've only been here a few days."

Timothy settled back, waiting for the information to more fully sink in. "What happened to your goodwill, lass? First, you tell him to find someone to help take care of him, and now that he has, it seems you're not so sure it was such a good idea."

"I didn't think it would be my best friend," she muttered, relieved that the foot massage was finally over. "She's not even Jewish!" was her futile rebuttal.

"Is that really so important?"

Rosalie thought for a moment, watching the two of them. David was reading his book again. Honey was laughing. Honey always had a great laugh. But then, Morris was a pretty funny guy.

"That's wonderful, David," Honey exclaimed, gathering up the tray. "Your story is coming along beautifully. Are you sure you're finished writing for today?"

David simply nodded as Honey carried the tray out into the kitchen. Then he closed his eyes for a moment. He could hear Honey cleaning up in the kitchen, running water in the sink, humming to herself. He thoughtfully leaned back in his chair, placing a half-typed page on the top of a pile that was growing and growing. The book was nearly finished.

David sighed a deep sigh as he gazed at Rosalie's picture framed in silver on a nearby table. He loved that picture. She was smiling that wonderful smile he so well remembered. His eyes briefly misted over. Now he had two women to inspire him, two women for whom to succeed. Rosalie was beginning to get the picture. She was still inspiring David but it was from another dimension—from the other side. Honey was inspiring David on earth.

"God knows she could use a husband," Rosalie was forced to concede. "She has to be twenty-seven. But she sure looks good," she admitted. "In fact, she looks terrific!"

"And there is Manuel," Timothy reminded her.

Rosalie's eyes misted over. For the moment she had forgotten Manuel—strong, handsome, wonderful Manuel. "He's an architect, David, and he writes poetry. You'd like him, David. He's a great guy." Rosalie's realization mixed the bitter with the sweet. It was sadness mixed with joy.

"You were a good husband, David. I should have told you that more often. I could have been a better wife. I shouldn't have nagged you so much. I was such a nudge. So—I'm sorry." But on second thought she added, "But maybe you needed a push now and then. Just maybe."

With that the picture on the screen faded out. David could no longer be seen. But at least Rosalie knew he would be all right. Time would heal his pain. In heaven time seemed to take longer, but with Manuel there it would be easier. It already was.

"It's hard looking at the past, present, and future all in the same moment," Rosalie confessed.

"One day it will not be so difficult," Timothy assured her. "You see, lass, you're weaving a vast tapestry and one day all the threads will finally be firmly in place. Then the picture will be complete. Till then, it's all just a matter of eternity."

Rosalie didn't respond. Instead, she went into the living room to stand before the large picture window. Over the lake the diminishing glow of sunset spread out in faint shades of pink and orange and lavender. Stars were beginning to twinkle, faintly shining. For a moment she had a fleeting recollection of the stars in the tunnel that, in turn, stirred an even deeper memory in the center of her soul—the memory of a million, billion lights brightly glittering in the firmament.

High above the lake a large white eagle glided in great circles on the shifting currents of air, free on the wing. She knew that her soul was as the eagle's. One day, she too, would take flight and soar.

So a year had passed on earth. She had grown in the passing. And David did need someone to love. Someone who could love him back. Someone who was a little crazy. Honey was a definite candidate in that respect. Rosalie smiled, remembering her best friend.

Honey had always liked David. Honey was a Cancer, very much the homebody. That was good for David. It was what he needed. Honey had always wanted children. So did David. Who could tell what their future together would bring? Only God really knew for sure. ✳

Chapter Fourteen

Manuel's mountaintop was enchanting. As far as the eye could see there was lush, fertile forest and an abundant variety of wildlife. Clear aqua glacier lakes dotted the countryside. Majestic snowcapped mountains could be seen higher still, the glory of nature.

Birds serenaded in the cedars and pines: saucy blue jays, bright cardinals, and robin redbreasts, to name but a few. The crispness of spring filled the air. The sun was bright in a deep blue sky where wispy clouds drifted on course. It was beautiful. Nature resplendent in variety of form, natural opulence uncluttered by civilization—the raw material of dreams.

A rushing mountain stream cascaded over sharp jutting rocks, creating an imposing waterfall that surged down smooth-faced cliffs for hundreds of feet. Far below a mighty river accepted the gift of increase, carrying it into the valley below, surging through rushing rapids and smooth coursing straits until it became a part of the great sea that was its destination. The stream had its song to sing. It was the song of water rushing home, persistent on its course. The rocks did not bruise the water on its perilous journey, but simply supplied variations on a theme. The theme was to continue, to go on and simply be. Growing in proportion as it was carried along the Stream of Life until the Mother Sea had taken back into herself that drop of moisture the Sun had called forth so many millennia ago. The sea eagerly and joy-fully received her own.

Together, Rosalie and Manuel watched the mighty stream cascading over sheer rock cliffs to join the river in its homeward course. They spoke with undines, the water spirits and nymphs who inhabited the streams and rivers and lakes, nurturing and guarding each in their charge.

At first, Manuel was apprehensive about introducing Rosalie to Aleatha. For in his eyes, she was the most stunning of the nymphs. Yet, all the undines were ethereal, wispy creatures of exquisite beauty, nearly transparent of form, yet capable of being seen by the eyes of souls in that dimension and sometimes by those on earth who were endowed with the gifts of the Spirit.

Felicia was Queen Undine in charge of the nymphs in that part of the kingdom. Her eyes were clear aqua blue, like the glacier lakes in her care. Her long, flowing hair of silver sparkled as though sprinkled with a host of tiny diamonds. Tiny droplets, crystalline in appearance, formed the crown upon her head. When sunbeams danced around her, they reflected from the points in her crown, bursting forth into a prism of lights, all hues of the rainbow.

Gregoria, her mate, was King of the Undines. His shining tunic was sapphire blue, edged in luminous silver, somewhat fluidic, like the waters over which he presided. He was especially admired and respected since he had been made Guardian of the Rainbows.

Where the great waterfall met and merged with the mighty river, an immense, perfectly formed rainbow beamed forth in vivid, dazzling colors. Rosalie was delighted and enchanted by every aspect of Manuel's mountaintop retreat. She also found it to be heaven.

Never before had she seen such splendid mountains, such verdant forest. She had been too involved with life in the city to take note of the wonders of nature the earth had provided for those with the eyes to see. Manuel was introducing her to another aspect of life, an aspect that helped quiet the mind and nourish the soul.

Rosalie met elves and gnomes, the nature spirits who guarded the forests, trees, and plants, and the mineral kingdom as well. Some reminded her of *Snow White and the Seven Dwarfs.* Yet there was no wicked witch and no one giving away poisoned apples in this forest. It made her wonder if the story had something to do with the serpent in the Garden of Eden. She also wondered when people would stop blaming women for all the ills in the world. At least the handsome prince had awakened Snow White from her death-like sleep. Perhaps that had something to do with man's role in awakening woman to her true purpose. Bits and pieces of truth were beginning to filter through and find meaning in her conscious awareness. Manuel had certainly awakened something magical inside Rosalie. He was opening her eyes to new horizons, new worlds—realities she had never before stopped to consider.

The elfin folk lived in a quaint village near Manuel's cabin. They looked much like human beings but were diminutive in stature. Most of them were slight in figure yet strong, with graceful, symmetrical features and a slight impish look about the eyes. The gnomes were sturdier, stockier types, somewhat lacking in the grace of the elves. They took care of the animals in the forest, and also took great pleasure in watching the water nymphs frolic. For as the nymphs moved they flowed, their delicate feet never touching the ground.

For the most part, elves and gnomes walked upon the ground like ordinary mortals. They were the guardians of the earth itself. Well known for being able to leap and jump great distances, sometimes in a single bound, they could disappear at will, like all the other nature spirits assigned to the different elements.

The gnomes especially enjoyed cooking up the herbs and nuts in abundance in the forest, making delicious ragouts and stews. They were never lacking in appetite, but always blessed whatever they ate, a custom adopted by mortals somewhere along the line. Rosalie was learning how all the kingdoms in Creation constantly interacted, serving as a check and balance to sustain the whole. Yet all were interdependent upon one another.

The elves and fairies loved to sing and dance. It was an essential part of their existence. They sang delightful songs about life in the forest, and told legendary tales about the ages past. There was a special name for each and every animal, tree, stone, and plant. Each blade of grass, each and every berry, nut, and flower were distinct and dear to them. There was even a name for each grain of sand that rested or rolled on multifarious shores. Such tenderness the earth spirits felt for their charges, such unconditional love.

Justin was chieftain amongst the elfin folk in that dimension. He had a sweet wife and sixteen adorable children, mostly boys. His wife was Leonora. She was bright and pert and pixie-like. Well over three hundred years old, she didn't look a day over thirty. Their clothes were colorful, mostly the hues of nature, reminiscent of the pictures presented in Irish folklore. Rosalie just knew that Timothy must feel very much at home here in the forest.

Rosalie and Manuel danced and dined with the elfin folk. Sometimes joining in a feast of hearty hazelnut and pine nut stew that included wild potatoes, succulent mushrooms, and forest asparagus seasoned with just enough thyme and sweet basil. They even learned their folk dances, dancing the night away with their wee friends in the fairy rings that flourished in the mountain meadow. Listening to fairies and gnomes sing their hearty or silly songs was a special delight. Or lending an ear to the elders as they recounted bold, captivating tales of long ago and of how there had been an awesome battle in their kingdom of nature. And of how, once the peace was restored, they were allowed to fully express their special gifts and keep the amazing treasures they had buried in many parts of the earth.

Manuel explained how the elfin folk were subhuman on the evolutionary scale. The clan in his forest had evolved to a station near that of humanity. Manuel had just begun to write stories about their humorous and adventurous encounters with human beings on the earth plane—mortals who were just beginning to awaken to the realization of life on a finer plane and the many different kinds of beings who dwelt there.

The elves inspired him to write poetry about the flowers and trees, and the undines to write sonnets about the rivers and streams. The nature spirits were helping Manuel refine his own special gifts and talents.

Rosalie watched and quietly listened. She talked less than she had talked for as long as she could remember. She was enchanted and delighted with Manuel's special place, for he was beginning to shed light in the dark corners of her consciousness. The fact was—he was turning out to be some prince.

Hand in hand, they took long walks together in the woods, quiet walks without words. Sometimes they sat beneath the noble trees serenaded by the music from the elfin village. At night they strolled beneath the glowing moon and twinkling stars, with fairy lanterns in the branches further illuminating the path before them. They joyously waded in crystal mountain streams; bubbling brooks of incandescent light washed away the sorrows of other lives, other times. Their love was being renewed. They were learning about one another and about themselves. Step by step, along the path they grew. Time seemed to stand still during those glorious moments in eternity, and yet, time was passing. Though for lovers, time is always eternity.

Rosalie never tired of sitting near the base of the immense waterfall with its rainbow spray overhead. Irving sat at her feet when he wasn't chasing butterflies in the meadow, though each time he was severely chastised by the elves, who could speak with all creatures. Once a friendly robin perched on Irving's back. Rosalie and Manuel were charmed, with Irving, with the robin, with the rainbow. But mostly, with each other.

Over time Manuel had become a good friend of Gregoria, Guardian of the Rainbows. He was a magnificent undine, tall and slender with golden hair and sea-green eyes. He usually wore a cloak of rainbow hues, flowing and grand. Upon his head he wore a crystal crown of dazzling brilliance. At first glance one might think him arrogant and proud, but Gregoria was neither. Conscious of the importance of his station, he simply knew everything there was to know about rainbows, and on that score he could afford to be proud.

Gregoria was teaching Manuel about color. Because of her own interest in painting, Rosalie was learning from him, too. She would sit in rapt attention as the two of them exchanged their knowledge and shared a special sort of camaraderie. Rosalie was learning the value of silence, though not without difficulty.

The water nymphs would giggle when Rosalie tended to chatter. She instinctively knew their laughter was harmless enough. It was all in good clean fun. The nymphs had taught her to swim in the deep pool at the bottom of the waterfall where the grandest of the rainbows began. They went skinny-dipping. Rosalie loved it. It made her feel so free, so unfettered. The nymphs were often childlike, even mischievous. She loved them like the little sisters she could not remember having.

Day became night and night day. Eternity was marking time. Then Timothy arrived. He had changed so much that neither of them recognized him at the outset.

"Top o' the morning," Timothy said in usual style. His voice was much the same, although younger. There was a look about him that was Timothy, but his hair was no longer white. It was medium brown, thicker and curlier. His face and body were that of a young man in his prime, early thirties at best. He was slim and trim and no longer looked anything at all like Santa Claus.

"Timothy O'Toole?" Rosalie cautiously inquired.

Timothy smiled. His face was still cherubic, just young Irish instead of old. His laughter had the very same lilt.

"Faith and begorra," Manuel affected his best Irish brogue, "What's happened to you, man? It looks like you've been drinking Irish whiskey from the fountain of youth."

"Just a touch," Timothy replied with a chuckle.

"What happened?" Rosalie was bewildered. "You don't look like a grandfather anymore. You're young and handsome. Look at you, Jesus!"

Rosalie had not changed all that much during her absence. So after making the proper adjustment in his energy field Timothy sat down on a fallen log, took a deep breath of fresh mountain air, and let out a long controlled sigh.

"Well, lass, I've been doing a bit of my homework. You see, being old was always a part of my consciousness, so when I got rid of the concept of myself as an aging gentleman and began seeing myself in my prime instead—well, here it is, and here I am. Amazing now, isn't it?"

Rosalie and Manuel nodded in agreement.

"Marcella kept telling me, over and over," he admitted. "It seems I wasn't really listening. But when I finally paid attention to what she was telling me, I did it." He slapped his thigh, announcing, "And now I'm feeling fit as a fiddle, I swear it. See for yourselves."

"And looking it, too," Manuel chimed in. "You planning on giving me any competition with my girl here?" He put a protective arm around Rosalie.

Timothy blushed, "Not me, lad. Just keep thinking of me as Santa Claus. Because you don't have to be old to give presents."

A tawny Irish setter bounded to Timothy's side, barking playfully. Irving pricked up both ears and jumped up on all fours, tail wagging. She might be twice his size, but she was a beauty. As the two dogs bounded off into the meadow, it was obvious Irving had a weakness for redheads.

"Penny looks great," Manuel remarked. "It looks like we may have another romance on our hands."

"You didn't introduce me," Rosalie teased.

"Aye, rest assured my Penny knows you without a proper introduction."

"You're something, Timothy O'Toole. You really are."

Rosalie was having a little trouble adjusting to his new self-image. It was almost like meeting a new person, yet his vibration was the same. Slowly, she was becoming more conscious of the vibratory subtleties surrounding her. Timothy did, however, seem a bit more vibrant.

"And you're something yourself, you are," he said, smiling. "Faith and begorra, you are!" And they all laughed together.

"So what brings you to our neck of the woods?" Manuel asked, handing Timothy a perfect apple.

"Well," he hedged and took a bite of apple, chewing in hearty approval. "Very good, very good indeed." He swallowed, then looked sheepish. "It seems to be time for Rosalie to return to Lakeside."

Manuel's expression became somber as Rosalie slipped both arms around his waist, snuggling up against him. Their time together in the mountains had been so very magical. Why in hell did she have to go now? Naturally, Timothy read their thoughts.

"I hear tell it's time for you to watch a bit of television," he informed her. "Life isn't just walking in the woods, you know. You're keeping Manuel here away from his drawing board."

"On, come on, Timothy," Manuel was trying to smile. "Do you have to spoil our fun?"

"Yeah," Rosalie protested. "Do you have to spoil our fun?"

Timothy stood there in silence. After all, he was on assignment. The choice was not his.

"Maybe I like the woods," Rosalie announced. "The woods are terrific, and so are the lakes and streams and meadows and waterfalls and rainbows, and undines and water nymphs and elves and gnomes and birds and bees that sing in the trees." She stopped to breathe. "And rivers and flowers and plants and all of the other animals that live in the forest. I petted Bambi. Now tell me that you can pet Bambi in Lakeside. Go on, tell me!"

Timothy didn't answer. He simply silently waited.

"Tell me that you can talk to fairies in Lakeside," she added, "and sing and dance in a fairy ring to a lute and a flute. Go on and tell me, already!"

"You do not have those circumstances in Lakeside," Timothy agreed. "But is that all there is? No offense to the fairy folk intended. They're some of my best friends. Back in Ireland we have a way with the wee folk. For you see, I met them long before I came here."

"I don't understand why I have to leave here," Rosalie said, sitting down beside Timothy on the fallen log. The look on her face was long and sad.

"It is time to get on with it, lass," Timothy said, gently taking her hand. "Manuel understands. He has been here a bit longer than you have."

The haunting refrain of the carousel could now be distantly heard—the magnificent carousel with its crystal unicorn, winged lion, and Pegasus. At first the melody sounded something like a music box that was running down, but then it picked up speed until it was playing faster and faster. The music was faint yet beckoning, beckoning to all to come join in the fun, beckoning for all to come take a ride on the glorious carousel with its shining brass ring that enticingly glittered in the light.

For a brief moment Rosalie could see the brass ring, the shiny brass ring just out of reach. She had missed it, just missed it. Yet somehow she knew that she would catch it one day.

"Maybe I do need to go back," she now relented. "I mean, Manuel hasn't taught me how to prune the roses yet."

✿

"Hey, I nearly forgot," Manuel declared, now all smiles. "And I can't break a promise to a beautiful lady, now can I?" For deep inside he understood. They couldn't stroll through the woods forever. If they did that, how could he ever become a great architect?

"Back to the drawing board," Manuel proclaimed, pulling Rosalie to her feet. Then he lifted her high into the air before he kissed her waiting lips.

"Listen, princess, tomorrow we will prune the roses. We'll have a great day. You'll see. Who knows, we may even have time for a ride on the carousel."

Their time together in the forest would soon be just a memory—like so many other experiences that they had shared. Rosalie so wanted to spend more time with Manuel on his mountain of the rainbow. And yet, deep inside she understood, while at the same time wondering why all good things had to turn into memories all too soon.

"So there will be room for more good things," Timothy told her, a faint smile upon his lips and a faraway look in his eyes.

"I'll buy that," Rosalie stated. "In fact, I'll take a dozen of them, forever and ever."

Timothy took her hands in his and quietly began, "Now close your eyes and think of Lakeside."

"I know. I know," she replied, smiling a smug smile.

Then closing her eyes, and mimicking Dorothy in the *Wizard of Oz*, Rosalie began repeating and repeating, "There's no place like home. There's no place like home. There's no place like home," and it worked! ✿

Chapter Fifteen

"I'll be damned!" Rosalie exclaimed, upon discovering that she was standing next to her recliner in Lakeside. "That is one of the weirdest things that's happened so far." She immediately sat down to quiet her vibrations while Timothy made himself comfortable on the sofa.

"When Manuel and I went to his mountain, this sort of thing kind of happened, but not nearly as fast. Just think how it would be if people on earth could travel like this. The oil and gas companies would be out of business in no time, and we wouldn't need airplanes or cars, buses, or trains; we wouldn't even need bicycles or roller skates. Good grief! That would put a lot of people out of work, Timothy. That would mean they would have to collect unemployment or find some other way to make a living. I mean, it could really screw up the economy."

"The earth plane will not be ready for travel at the speed of thought for some time yet," Timothy assured her. "Once it is ready, the adjustment for all souls will be relatively simple. Try not to worry about such things, my dear, for everything is evolving as it should evolve and at just the right pace."

It was too much for her to think about, so Rosalie simply went to the kitchen to satisfy a sudden urge for apple pie. Right in the middle of the kitchen table she found a freshly baked apple pie with a note from Aunt Beatrice, who could obviously read minds, too.

"Isn't she sweet," Rosalie exclaimed, taking two plates out of the cupboard.

There was also hot coffee. Heaven could certainly be accommodating. Rosalie cut two generous portions of pie and poured coffee into mugs before returning to the den. Once there she sat down and stared at the now blank television screen.

"It's a shame they put so many televisions in this house. I mean, this is the only one we watch. This is one of my favorite rooms in the house."

"I'm rather fond of it myself," Timothy confessed. "But what you do need to realize is there is nothing miserly about the Source. The Source is abundance. It's the same on earth actually. It just takes a bit of time for most souls to learn and truly grasp that truth, let alone put it into positive action. When we're living in a physical body we can be so dense and so impatient. Glory be to the Father! It's the third dimension, earth life. Time, space, and patience."

Rosalie was enjoying her apple pie. It was truly delicious. Timothy was such a dear, always teaching, letting her in on the grand scheme of things. It still required some adjustment on her part to see him the way he was now, so young and vital. Yet she was happy to be with him again regardless of how he looked. She had become accustomed to the feel of him, to his energy. Timothy felt good to Rosalie, very comfortable.

"If I have to go back to earth again, it would be really nice if you came along. Think of all the fun we could have together. Is there any way that could be officially arranged?" she asked.

He wondered if Rosalie had been reading his mind. Her giggle gave him his answer. They laughed at the same time.

"You're coming right along, you are," Timothy acknowledged, rather pleased. "Me and you on earth together, wouldn't that be something?"

"That would be terrific!" Rosalie's eyes misted over as she added, "As long as Manuel came, too, of course."

"Ah, but of course," Timothy heartily agreed. "We couldn't go back without Manuel, now could we?"

"Actually, I don't like going anywhere without Manuel. And yet I have this powerful conviction deep down inside of me that Manuel is really part of me. Which means—wherever I go, I take him along with me. Like he's always in my thoughts every minute all the time, so I can never really go anywhere without him anyway. It's a very strange thing to explain, Timothy. Like even when he's not around he is, and part of me is always with him wherever he might be. Am I making any sense to you at all?"

"Aye, lass," he replied, his eyes filled with understanding. "Very good sense, indeed."

That was when music started coming from the television, an easily identifiable refrain: *The Bridal March*. And there on the screen was a beautiful bride marching down the aisle of a modest church on her father's arm. She was wearing an old-fashioned ivory lace wedding gown with a high neck. Delicate seed pearls were clustered in the design of a rose on the bodice. A long train trailed along behind her. Due to the veil, Rosalie could not see her face. She was not paying attention to the small crowd seated on either side of the aisle. All Rosalie could see was David standing at the altar waiting for his bride.

The minister stood just behind David. His brother, Kenny, was standing to the side. David and Kenny were dressed in black tuxedos. Rosalie had never seen David in a tux before. When they were married he wore a brown suit that was three years old. He hadn't worn lilies of the valley on his lapel either, only a carnation.

Rosalie stared hard at the back of the bride who was now standing next to David before the minister. The ceremony was about to begin.

"He's no rabbi!" Rosalie lamented, sitting forward, tension mounting. "He's a minister—a Christian minister!"

Rosalie jumped up and started pacing. "Myrna Rosenberg must be having a heart attack this very minute. Get ready for new recruits!"

"He's a Unitarian minister," Timothy quietly pointed out. "Nice chap, hear tell. I have it on the best authority."

"Unitarian?" Rosalie moaned, shaking her head. "Poor Myrna." Again she paced, wringing her hands. "How can you do this to your mother, David?" she screamed at the television, "with me dead only a year! Are you crazy? Do you want to give your mother a total nervous breakdown?"

The father of the bride now turned back the veil. Rosalie had a clear view. The bride was Honey. Honey's green eyes were misty as she turned to David. David looked nervous. But Rosalie could see the love in David's eyes. She knew that look. It was love for Honey. Honey's eyes reflected equal love for David.

"I'll be damned! She nailed him. And me her best friend." Rosalie sat down and took another bite of apple pie, thinking it might help remove the lump she felt in her throat. Tears filled her eyes. "She makes a pretty bride, don't you think?" she asked, sniffling, trying for nonchalance as tears rolled down both cheeks.

"Very pretty," Timothy carefully conceded. "And David makes a very handsome groom."

"Unitarian," Rosalie muttered. "David's father must be turning over in his grave right now. And his mother, she must be pulling her hair out in handfuls. I didn't know Honey was Unitarian, for Chrissake. What in the hell is Unitarian?"

"For one thing they believe in religious freedom," Timothy informed her. "They're essentially Christian, though somewhat unorthodox." He saw Rosalie wince at his remarks, but he continued just the same, "One of their main aims is to unite the world in brotherhood."

"Lots of luck," Rosalie replied with a shrug.

That was when she noticed the Star of David hanging around David's neck on a fine gold chain. It was larger than the one she had given him for his birthday two years before she died.

"It's his wedding gift from Honey," Timothy ventured. "She wants to support him in his religious beliefs. Besides, the Star of David is an ancient symbol for love."

"I know," Rosalie said, feeling rather sad. "The main reason I wanted him to wear it was because he's a David and David means *Beloved*. That was why I bought it for him." Tears flowed down both her cheeks. "And he was my beloved—once."

David and Honey were exchanging gold wedding bands. The time came for the groom to kiss the bride. Tears rolled down both of Honey's cheeks. She had finally made it, Rosalie thought. She was a married woman and she had to cry about it?

Just before David kissed Honey he tenderly touched her tears with his fingertips, brushing them away. His gesture was so tender, so loving. Rosalie started to sniffle. As David kissed his bride Rosalie blew her nose. Then brightly smiling, David and Honey marched back down the aisle as husband and wife. The wedding reception would be taking place in the garden.

Rosalie just sat there, staring. There were mixed emotions inside her, tugging at her heart. She felt happy and sad at the same time. The sort of sadness many people feel at weddings. Sadness mixed with doubt, with fear, with hopes and dreams all mixed up together.

"I hope they'll be happy. I really mean it," Rosalie said and blew her nose again. "But couldn't they have waited just a little while longer? I haven't been gone all that long."

"Two years," Timothy stated.

"Two years?" Rosalie repeated. "Time sure does fly. I mean, blink your eye, and it's gone. Two whole years?" She quickly calculated in her mind. "She must be twenty-seven. She was four years younger than me."

Rosalie began checking out the reception line. Just as she thought, Myrna Rosenberg was not at the wedding. Poor Myrna. David had married a tea leaf-reading Gentile in a Unitarian church. How could his mother ever speak to him again? Poor David, with the wrath of that woman hanging over him. She might forgive him on her deathbed, yet. But knowing Myrna Rosenberg, she would probably hold out until the very last breath. What if there were grandchildren? Could she ignore her own grandchildren, her own flesh and blood? Poor David, his mother would make his life hell.

David took out a cigarette and lit up.

"Look at that!" Rosalie cried out, pointing. "David quit smoking two months before I died. Two whole months! He's gone to hell since I left. David is smoking a cigarette!"

Timothy restrained himself, deciding to leave well enough alone.

"David, you know you shouldn't smoke." She was standing close to the TV, screaming in his face, "You're too high-strung, David. You know it only makes you more nervous, so put it out, already! Put it out!"

David took a long hard look at the cigarette and was about to discard it when, all of a sudden, his expression became very determined and he defiantly took another puff.

"How do you like them apples? Here I am telling him something for his own good and there he is, defying me. Honey MacIntosh gets her hands on him for a couple of years and he goes and starts smoking again and gets married in a Unitarian church. What's next?"

"He has finished his book," Timothy quietly mentioned, a pleased expression on his face.

"Big deal!" She was wrapped up in watching David smoke that cigarette. Then she noticed Nancy, his sister-in-law, talking to Honey. Nancy was wearing a pretty dress of aqua lace. She looked nice.

"She had a boy!" Rosalie just knew, even before she saw the energetic toddler hanging onto his father's hand.

"And she's pregnant again yet! Doesn't she know there's a population explosion on earth? What's with those two? Have they forgotten what they know about birth control?"

Rosalie suddenly knew so many things all at once that she was amazed. Kenny and Nancy Rosenberg would have four children, two boys and two girls in that exact order. He was a plumber. Plumbers could get rich in Los Angeles. It cost forty bucks to fix a toilet. Rosalie guessed he could afford a big family. Anyway, in a couple of years he would have his own business. Kenny would do fine. He would make lots of money.

"How come I suddenly know so much just like that?" she snapped her fingers.

"Your consciousness is expanding," Timothy told her. "In this dimension the future is easier to see. When you're on that side it can be a bit more difficult."

"No kidding?" She was delighted. "So David sold his book. That's terrific!"

"No, that will happen in six months," Timothy interjected, "after considerable revision. The present publisher will offer him a contract with some stipulations. David will take his time to think it over. He'll do a rewrite, and in the end he'll sell it to another publisher who will make him a much better deal."

"So David really is a writer." She was pleased as punch. "How about that? Did I help to make it happen, Timothy? Did I help him in any way at all?"

"Of course, you did. You helped David renew his confidence in his material and himself."

"Did Morris get away with it?" she had to ask. For some reason she couldn't see how the story ended.

"Morris is forced to make restitution," Timothy acknowledged. "Morris also realizes that the world will not change simply because he wants it to. But in the end, he becomes more confident. He becomes a lobbyist in Washington, D.C., working to block horrors like germ warfare from being produced by any company or government in the world. Morris, of course, is a valiant idealist. The world could use far more souls just like him."

"Morris is one of David's alter egos," Rosalie confessed. "Deep down inside, David Rosenberg would like to do things like that—meaningful, spectacular things that would help people and the world to change for the better. But he's too shy to do it himself, so he has to have Morris to do it for him."

"David will write other books with a message. That's how he can share his philosophy without sticking his neck out too far," Timothy affirmed. "Perhaps he will become less shy and more courageous in voicing his beliefs that way. His writing is sure to do good along the way. Much stranger things have happened on earth."

"I'm so glad that David is going to be a successful writer. No more vacuum cleaners, huh?"

"Not if he keeps following his dream," Timothy seemed to hedge just a touch.

"You mean you don't have all the answers, Timothy?" Rosalie was fascinated and amused.

"Good heavens, no!" was his indignant response. "Souls have the gift of free will. Individual determination makes the difference. All humanity is endowed with the Divine Spark of the Creator. When we recognize the Creator as the First Cause, all things become possible for us."

Rosalie's attention was drawn back to the television screen. Old and new friends were congratulating the groom and kissing the bride. Honey's mother, Mary, made a radiant mother of the bride. She was so thrilled about the wedding. She had waited a long time for this special moment. Honey's parents were making lots of new friends and having a great time.

"Honey's grandmother on her mother's side was born in County Cork," Rosalie informed Timothy. "She has a cousin in Ireland who runs a tavern in Cork that has been in the family well over a hundred years."

"Is that a fact now?" Timothy sat forward, his fork poised in mid-air. "Lovely woman, Mary MacIntosh. It seems she married a Scot." He was checking out their energy fields. "Nice parents she has, right lovely folk."

"Her father has a liquor store in San Francisco, so you could say he's in the spirits business, too, right, Timothy?" Rosalie said with a smile. "I've always liked Honey's parents. They're so nice. However, I'm not so sure how happy they are about their daughter marrying a Jew in a Unitarian church. Martin MacIntosh was raised Presbyterian, but Mary is Catholic."

"Is that a fact now?" Timothy was pursing his lips and narrowing his eyes. "Well, now, they don't seem to mind that much. I mean, her father giving her away and all, and her mother seems to be having herself a fine time." Timothy paused a beat before he asked, "Is Mary a practicing Catholic?"

"How would I know? Check her out," Rosalie retorted with a shrug.

The bride and groom were feeding each other wedding cake and drinking champagne through linked arms. A small band of musicians started to play. Honey and David began dancing the first dance, gazing into each other's eyes, with everyone looking on so very pleased. The scene was so typical. Yet for a brief moment, Rosalie found herself there with them in the garden, magnetically drawn to them as they danced around the floor. It was then that the haunting tune of the carousel began to play in her mind. And in a flash she saw the brass ring reflecting tiny beams of light. Deep inside her was a strange, warm sensation, a special tingling that made her smile.

"Do you think they'll have children?" she felt the need to ask.

Timothy, too, began to hear the music of the carousel and saw the brass ring. "What was Mary's maiden name?" he cautiously inquired.

"I think Honey once told me it was McKenna. Why?"

"A second cousin on my mother's side married a McKenna. Isn't that interesting though?" A warm feeling now welled up inside him.

Again Rosalie felt a strange pull toward the happy couple. A peculiar though familiar sensation stirred mixed emotions deep inside her.

Honey now wore a yellow cotton dress. David was wearing an off-white sport shirt and tan slacks. He looked nice, but Rosalie couldn't help noticing that his hair was starting to gray. After all, he had to be thirty-two. Time was marching on for David Rosenberg.

Rosalie thought that Honey would make a good mother. She would bake cookies for her children and give them cookies and milk. She might even teach them to read tea leaves. David would probably be a good father. But she thought he might make a poor disciplinarian. He could be such a pussycat when it came to standing his ground. And David could be so high-strung. Kids just might get on his nerves.

Beneath a shower of rice, Honey and David hurried to get into a white Datsun. Vacuum cleaner sales had to be up. But then, Honey was a schoolteacher, her money would help. And David would publish his book. People might even buy it. That would be terrific.

The Datsun eventually pulled into a Holiday Inn. The honeymoon would take place in Mission Bay, San Diego. Big deal, Rosalie thought. David had taken her to Carmel. Carmel was romantic. What was romantic about Mission Bay in San Diego?

David and Honey entered a large room with a king-sized bed. David was nervous. All Rosalie could see was the king-sized bed. Honey was nervous. She went over to the window to look out at all the boats in the bay, and to watch the twinkling lights reflected in the water. David tipped the bellboy two dollars. Big spender! It was his last two singles.

Now Rosalie was nervous. Once more she heard the haunting music of the carousel—louder, clearer, more distinct—as David walked over to the window and slipped his arms around Honey's waist. Honey seemed to melt. She sighed in contentment, hugging David's arms more tightly around her. David nuzzled her neck, planting tiny kisses one after the other.

Rosalie got goose bumps. She shivered. So did Timothy. They were definitely getting romantic, even if it was San Diego. Rosalie was transfixed as David turned Honey around to face him. He kissed her, sweetly, tenderly, and deliciously. Rosalie's heart began to beat faster. Timothy was getting nervous. He swallowed with difficulty. The kisses were becoming longer, more intense, more involved, more passionate by the minute. Rosalie swallowed with difficulty.

David started unzipping the back of Honey's dress and the screen went blank.

"Damn!" Rosalie exclaimed, a sheepish grin on her face as she turned to Timothy who was fanning himself. Then she turned back to the blank television screen.

"So what happened?" she demanded.

"No prying allowed," was Timothy's explanation, an edge in his voice as he spoke.

"But it's just life," Rosalie insisted. "I mean, it's what makes the world go round and round and round."

The music of the carousel began to build, growing louder and louder and louder, faster and faster and faster, until all at once it stopped. Everything became silent and still.

"Wouldn't that be something?" Rosalie remarked. "Half Scotch-Irish and half-Jewish, you and me, Timothy. We could go back as their children. Wouldn't that be something?" There was a serious tone to her voice and a gleam in her eyes.

"Yes," Timothy agreed, his voice just above a whisper. "That would be something!" He shivered. He couldn't help it.

So did Rosalie. ✳

Chapter Sixteen

Back on the mountain among the towering cedars and pines, Manuel was standing near the thundering waterfall, staring at the place where Rosalie and Timothy had disappeared from view. Vanished into thin air, as a matter of fact, a common occurrence in that dimension of reality. Irving and Penny disappeared right along with them, for they were a part of their special soul patterns.

The nature spirits in the forest were prone to doing that sort of thing, disappearing, more often than not without warning. Poof and they were gone, like brilliant, dancing sparklers miraculously extinguished. Sometimes a glimmer of iridescent light remained, making it hard to tell whether they were still present in their etheric form or had dashed off to another part of the galaxy in response to a special need or passing whim—especially the air sylphs and undines, who were such nebulous creatures to begin with.

Manuel was in a dreamy state of reverie, minding his own business, when his heart and solar plexus suddenly filled with a distinct yet inexplicable longing for New York City. It was unmistakable, an undeniable nostalgia for that particular city. A powerful, persistent yearning for everything New York had ever been or ever represented in any shape or form. He was overcome by an irresistible urge to see skyscrapers, to ride subways, to see the Empire State

Building just one more time. To buy burnt pretzels from street vendors in Manhattan and explore the open air markets in Brooklyn. To visit his old neighborhood in the Bronx.

Manuel yearned to ride through the Lincoln Tunnel in the peak of rush hour, to hang out on Coney Island in the heat of July. It was an unexplainable yet undeniable sensation that enveloped his entire being. Bizarre, he thought, all things considered. After all, he had just enjoyed a sensational time with Rosalie right there on his mountain, romping with gnomes in the woods. Singing under sycamores, cedars, and pines, and dancing with elves in magical fairy rings. Splashing in lakes and streams with undines, who were simply the best when it came to frolicking, whirling and twirling through waterfalls and rushing rapids.

His time with Rosalie was unique, extraordinary. What on earth could bring about this unexpected longing for New York City? This sudden desire to return to the clamor, the filth, the noise, the crime, the violence? The ethnic class struggles for survival and dominance? The cut-throat tactics and competition to get to the top? The sibling rivalry for familial acceptance and overall demands of life on the planet that he had left far behind him not so very long ago? He actually yearned to return to life on earth. Why, he asked himself? For the very life of him, Manuel could not even begin to figure it out.

Before he even had time to consider the mysterious feelings and longings sweeping over and through him, he realized that he was beginning to dematerialize. A giddy lightheadedness set in as he rematerialized and found himself standing in the middle of a grand alabaster temple on a cliff, high above a restless, ever-churning sapphire sea. Beside him was a large marble statue of some guy who looked very much like a Greek god. This was a new experience for Manuel. He had never been here before—except the place vaguely reminded him of somewhere he might have been once upon a time.

He was rather impressed with the twelve towering pillars evenly spaced in a large circle all around him. They held up a spiraling ceiling ornately carved with scenes from the Greek Pantheon. He didn't recognize all the various signs and symbols so magnificently displayed, though his present and past interest in the architectural wonders of the ancient and modern world made some of it familiar. Deep inside his soul he still had questions about the legendary accounts of ancient Greece and Crete. He wasn't sure where to separate fact from fiction.

His attention was then drawn to the flickering flame burning steadily in front of him. A combination of blue, red, and yellow glowed and danced up through an opening edged in glistening gold scallops in the center of the marble floor—twelve scallops, just like the twelve pillars of the temple.

As Manuel gazed into the blazing flame of celestial fire, faint memories began to stir. Recollections arose that became stronger and stronger. They were memories of ancient Greece and of his once-beloved Macedonia. A multitude of images streamed through his consciousness. He attempted to arrest the visual torrent racing before his inward vision. Mentally, he reached out, and in that instant he became completely absorbed in that which he had only been observing.

He found himself seated astride a powerful gray steed. On his head was a finely tooled helmet of brass and steel. An ornate breastplate strapped to his torso displayed the same family crest as the helmet. Thick leather leggings protected the taut, sweaty muscles of his legs. He steadily held the horse's reins in his hand. Skillfully disciplined horseflesh quivered beneath him in eager anticipation of a battle to be fought and won. The fearless horse valiantly carried his heroic warrior to their mutual destiny of a clash of clinging broadswords. Miraculously, horse and man somehow survived one more terrible skirmish.

Manuel could feel the sweat. He could smell the blood and death of the battle scene as adrenalin mixed with blood surged through his arteries and veins, throbbing in his head, and pulsating through his distended temples. The shouts and cries of the wounded and dying were deafening all around him. Then, all at once, they were all again ghostly sounds and ghostly images from another time and place in the history of his soul. Altogether, he found it a most disconcerting experience.

First, Rosalie had gone off, evaporating with Timothy. Then he'd disappeared from his forest to find himself in a marble temple he had never seen before. And then, just from staring at some flickering flame, he had found himself experiencing the terrors and excitement of hand-to-hand combat against an enemy he couldn't see or hear or even begin to completely remember. Obscure demons and ghostly opponents had risen up to haunt the dim corridors of his consciousness, curious beings that were there yet not there, at least not lately.

As Manuel diverted his gaze from the flickering flame, he was once more aware of his Grecian surroundings. He was conscious of the sound of the mighty ocean fearlessly throwing itself against the sharp rocks far below in brilliant proclamation of its divine right and purpose—a purpose eternally fulfilled by divine decree. That was when he heard the melodious music of a lute blending with the sweet notes of a flute. It was when he sensed the gentle breeze that was blowing all around him. A breeze that caressed him from head to toe, dissolving his tension and fear, a sweet-scented breeze that seemed to heal his very soul.

When he turned he found her standing there, the magnificent, mysterious, exquisite Marcella. How silly of him not to realize it was her temple from the outset. Everything suddenly made sense. For a moment her beauty overwhelmed him. Whenever he saw her, even briefly, Marcella took his breath away and left him speechless, mindless.

Manuel was even more in awe of Marcella than his good friend Timothy was.

Twice before they had met, but never here in her own splendid, grand element—her way station, as it was known. Most souls spoke of her temple in reverent, hushed tones. Here in this place she was known to counsel souls suspended between dimensions.

There was lots of speculation as to who Marcella really was, of course, at least in Manuel's neck of the woods. Most souls had not reached a level where they could actually understand, for most souls found it nearly impossible to discern anything at all about those presiding at a higher frequency. Manuel realized that something very special was about to take place. A visit from Marcella always portended an extraordinary event or set of circumstances. For the moment, he just silently stood there drinking in her ethereal beauty, her magnificent energy—her Divine Love.

Marcella understood everything that was happening. She knew Manuel could use an additional dose of awe at that time, something that never hurts, now and again, during the evolution of a soul. Awe was an excellent sentiment for uplifting the human spirit.

"Welcome to my temple, Manuel," she proclaimed as she walked toward him.

He remained silent as he stood there watching her. He was searching his mind for an adequate response. She made him feel like a little boy who had been caught with his hand in the cookie jar, although it certainly had not been his idea to show up here.

"Nice place you have here," he finally managed, feeling like a ninny. "Terrific...architecture." He had a silly smile on his face. He knew she could see right through him. There was no kind of game he could play with this lady, so naturally, he was nervous and feeling more than a little awkward. He had no idea what to expect next.

Marcella was wearing her usual diaphanous white gown and sapphire-blue cape. Her wispy blonde hair was piled high on her head and reflected tiny beams of sparkling light. Manuel thought her hair was studded with little diamonds or crystals. Yet he also knew that celestial beings could do just about anything they wanted to with atoms and molecules. In all probability, these souls could make anything sparkle. They knew more about Creation and manifestation than anyone he had ever been privileged to meet. Knowing these souls had that kind of knowledge and awareness gave him a sense of comfort and a deep sense of peace.

Marcella was observing Manuel with a whimsical smile on her face, much like a mother observing a child in its struggle to appear more grown up. Not that she had an attitude. Marcella was never condescending. She was caring, loving, like a mother watching a toddler trying to coordinate his fingers to tie his shoes. The mother could always tie the shoe herself and be done with it, but the child would never know the true satisfaction that came with achievement. The child would never learn how it felt to win. Marcella understood a great deal. Souls needed to lose a few times before they could win. Souls needed compassion and humility. They needed to know all the differences or the moment of exhilaration and exultation would never come, and they would never hear the angels sing on account of their triumph.

"Your brother Juan has retired from the fire department," Marcella told Manuel, simply and straightforwardly.

"Is that right?" Manuel responded in surprise. Juan was his eldest brother. To Manuel's knowledge he had never married. "Good for him. That's great."

"Several years ago Juan married a widow with three young children," she continued. "Her husband was killed in a fire on the Lower East Side when a ceiling collapsed. He had been a fireman as well. Your brother embraced the children as his own. He has enjoyed a good life with Maria.

Sometime ago he adopted the children. Their eldest son, Marcos, is currently in his third year of college, Columbia. He's very bright."

Manuel had never bothered to check in on Juan. He had always felt competitive with him. He had been jealous of him because Juan had a job with the city that took him far away from the family. A job he enjoyed. A job that gave him a sense of freedom and purpose. Mama had not held on to Juan so tightly. Not the way she had held on to Manuel— the Sierra stranglehold for dear life.

"What about Hector?" Manuel asked. "Did he ever marry that pretty model he was so crazy about?"

Marcella smiled and replied, "No, Manuel. I'm sure that even you could see it was not their destiny to remain together for long."

"You're right on that score. She was much too uptown for sweet Hector. But he sure was crazy about that woman. He's all right, isn't he?"

"Look within your heart, Manuel. You can discover the truth there for yourself."

Manuel tried to focus within his heart, but he just wasn't getting it. He was not making contact with Hector.

"Hector is doing fine," she finally said. "You need to try a little harder, Manuel. If you can just learn to focus you will know everything you need to know without having to be told. From this level it can be rather simple." She watched, waiting for him to follow her suggestion. Marcella had faith in Manuel.

For a moment, Manuel just stood there, questioning his capacity to tune in on the family he had left on earth. He knew better than to question Marcella. She was always right, so he closed his eyes and began to look within. He began to examine his heart, concentrating his full attention on Hector. Dear, sweet Hector. And soon he could see him. In his mind's eye he could see his brother, the one who had been four years younger than he was. He could see Hector now.

For a short time, Hector had been his archrival with Mama. Hector was the one to receive Mama's special favors, her undivided attention, but not for long. It was only for a short time, for after Hector came Rosa, then Carlos, and finally Theresa. By the time Theresa arrived, Manuel had learned to cope with lack of attention from Mama. He had entered the major leagues when it came to sibling rivalry. Besides, he was twenty-two.

All together there were six Sierra children, from three to six years apart in age. Manuel was number two. He was not the baby for long. While he was growing up, Manuel learned to channel his pent-up frustrations and jealousies into playing baseball and basketball. He also learned how to shout—at the other team and at his teammates on the floor or in the field, instead of shouting at his brothers and sisters. It made things much more peaceful at home. It made it a lot easier to deal with Mama and her demanding ways. Manuel never really understood why Mama always expected so much more from him than she seemed to expect from the other boys in the family. A long time ago it had dawned on him that maybe, just maybe, somewhere in the back of her mind Mama knew that he wouldn't be with her all that long. He could never be sure that was the real reason and doubted there was any way he would know for sure.

Manuel discovered that his brother Hector was now married to a girl nicknamed Chili who came from Ecuador. Her hair was bleached a luminous platinum. Her curvaceous figure was a clue to her name. That chick had to be hot. They had two kids and another on the way. Hector was working at a bank and had recently been promoted. Hector was doing fine, although it seemed that in time his Chili might burn more than his palate. She was showy, just like all the other girls Hector had ever been attracted to, but she did seem to love the guy. And they seemed to be having a good time. They gave their kids a whole lot of love.

Manuel's attention now returned to Marcella. "I see what you mean. He's okay, my little brother. He's doing all right."

"You already know about Rosa," she said, an understanding smile on her face.

"Rosa married a Greek violinist. I guess nobody keeps secrets from you? Is that how it is?" He suddenly felt shy and self-conscious in her presence.

Marcella silently watched and waited.

"I was always closer to my sisters," he admitted. "What about my little brother, Carlos? He was already a ladykiller at fifteen. He must be pushing thirty by now."

"Close your eyes and look within," was her only reply.

"Come on," Manuel protested, "This can't be the only reason you brought me here. Why don't you tell me the real reason that I'm here?"

"You haven't asked about Theresa yet." She watched him, awaiting the natural unfolding of destined events.

Theresa had been his favorite. His baby sister. She was only ten years old when he was killed in the city. She was devastated by the news and took it very badly. Manuel was her big, brave, handsome brother, the one who protected her from all the teasing by the neighborhood gangs. The one who kept everybody in line. The one who talked to her teachers and the principal when Mama claimed she had too much to do to bother. Manuel would take care of it. Manuel would straighten things out—Manuel—always Manuel. Papa was always off mowing lawns and trimming hedges on Long Island. Papa worked long hours. Papa needed to make money to feed the family, to pay the rent, to keep a roof over their heads, to put clothes on their backs. Manuel could handle it, always Manuel.

Manuel had always been there whenever Theresa needed him. He was the one who helped her with her homework. The one who explained why the kids at school were so mean. It was always Manuel who made her feel better, who made the big, bad bogeymen go away. Who named her goldfish and never forgot to feed them. Who played with her in the park on Sunday afternoons.

When Manuel died so suddenly and unexpectedly, it left a big hole in Theresa's life. Her other siblings did everything they could to make the hole smaller, to make it less frightening—less terrible for a little girl who had lost her favorite brother, her best friend, and the only real hero she had ever known. The heartache experienced by Theresa due to his presumably premature departure still distressed Manuel. She had cried so much. She just cried and cried and cried, day after day, sobbing herself to sleep at night for months and months, for years.

Manuel tried to close his eyes and look deep within. For some strange reason, he just wasn't up to it. He remembered Theresa with such tenderness, such longing, his beautiful, little Theresa with her long, dark, shining black hair, and her deep, dark, questioning brown eyes. Theresa was the one who always asked why the sky was blue, the one who wanted to know what made the sun stay in place. She was the one who wanted to know where rain came from and why it left. She was his dear little sister, who prayed for him every night and solemnly lit candles in church every week, hoping against hope that one day the two of them would see each other again, that they would be together yet one more time.

Then suddenly, the truth washed over his entire being. His sister, Theresa, had married an Italian from Brooklyn, Antonio Valenti. Theresa was not a baby anymore. She was twenty-four and pregnant. Theresa and Antonio were expecting their first child. Theresa had been praying for a son. Now Manuel knew why he was there. He understood the purpose for his meeting with Marcella.

Naturally, Marcella was partially responsible for his receiving the full story—the full impact of the impending drama on earth. It was her task to present Manuel with the facts, to circumspectly—though lovingly—inform him of all the angles. Manuel needed to make a fair and just decision.

"The time has come for you to make your choice," she told him, looking fully into his soul.

Manuel stared at Marcella. His mind was a blank. Once more he was speechless, bewildered. The full implication of her words reverberated throughout his being. His aura began flashing, streaming in brilliant rays of iridescent light. Visions of Rosalie ran through his consciousness. The mere thought of leaving her now tore at his heart and soul. What could he do? What would he do? About Theresa? About Rosalie—sweet, wonderful Rosalie, the soul he loved so much? The one he had only so recently found again after such a very long time. The one who was so much a part of his very being?

During their most recent lives on earth both of them had been born in New York. They had lived in different parts of the same city in the same period of time but had never met, not even once, not even for a moment. How could he leave her now? His Rosalie, his festival of roses? How could he lose sight of her so soon and for how long? For how many centuries? What was he to do? Theresa was praying. He could hear her praying that very moment.

"Rosalie will soon be faced with a similar decision," Marcella announced. She knew his questions before he could ask them, a distinct advantage from her perspective.

Manuel blankly stared into the eternally burning flame. He was searching his mind and his heart for some kind of answer, any answer. There was none plainly in sight.

"There is only so far the two of you can progress at your present level," Marcella revealed. "You are at a place in your evolution where you need the experiences of earth life to reap full soul growth and development. Besides, it is the task of mortal men and women in the present dispensation of time to bring heaven down to earth. The earth itself is ready to evolve into a new state of being greater than anything it has previously known. There will soon be a great leap in consciousness."

Marcella walked past him to face the open sea. Her sapphire-blue cape woven with gold billowed out behind her, whirling and dancing in the wind. For a long moment she stood with her face turned toward the radiating light.

"You have desires, Manuel," she continued, her voice compassionate, "dreams and aspirations that can only be fulfilled upon the earth." She kept her face partially toward the light before finally turning to fully face him. "Your time of preparation here is nearly at an end. There is work to be done, a job for you on earth. Naturally, there is karma, debts to be collected and paid, unfinished lessons to be learned with the family you left behind you. There are many loose ends in the tapestry of your life.

"And yet, it is for you to decide whether you will fulfill the promise made to Theresa so long ago to return as her son, or to linger here a while longer, thereby changing the cycle for everyone concerned, including your beloved Rosalie. Ultimately, it is your decision, Manuel. Yours alone."

"You make it sound so serious," Manuel finally said, feeling overwhelmed, confused. "You make it sound as though I personally can change the course of history, single-handedly."

"We can all change the course of history, Manuel, each and every moment," she was looking directly into his eyes. "Changing the course of history is always within the range of possibility for all souls who choose to make a difference. Those who have developed enough character and skill are able to take a stand and change the course of history for the better, whether upon the earth or in some other system. History has been changed—for better or for worse—throughout the ages. Fortunately for all of us, it has been mostly for the better."

Marcella slowly walked back to the center of the temple and stood beside the statue of Matthias near the eternally burning flame. She was calm and collected, so self-assured.

"How long do I have to make my decision?" he was almost afraid to ask.

"You have until tomorrow," was her calm reply.

Manuel released a long sigh and wearily sat down on a marble bench to try to steady his anxious energy field. He put his hands to his head and pressed. He tried to breathe slowly. For all his effort he could not clearly see into his future. He sat there silently shaking his head, staring into the brilliantly flickering flame. Images of Rosalie and Theresa intermittently rose up before him, fleeting back and forth, in and out of his mind, in and out of his heart in warm, pulsating waves. How for the life of him could he choose between these two women? Two women he loved, each in a different yet important way. His love was deep. His love was real. His love was unconditional.

"I cannot tell you of the Hierarchy's plan for your life on earth until you inform me of your decision at first light. Your guardian is ready to accompany you on your return. We are confident about your architectural gift, and your writing skills have improved to the point where you should be able to make a significant contribution. I await your decision at first light, at which time there will be further information given to you. I trust your response to the call of destiny will be just and equitable for all concerned. Most of all for your own soul." And with that she was gone in a whirling flash of brilliant light that spiraled up and out of the center of the temple into the seeming vastness of the universe.

In an instant Manuel was standing back in his forest near the edge of the cascading waterfall on his mountain, close to the place where the magnificent rainbow began. With God's help and his own fair measure of wisdom, Manuel's fate would be decided by first light. 🌸

Chapter Seventeen

Throughout the day Manuel patiently taught Rosalie the essentials for pruning roses. Fading blossoms needed to be cut back to a five-leaf stem, five being the number of rose petals at the base. Five was the number of the physical senses and the number for Humanity. The five-pointed star was the Star of Humanity. It was sometimes known as the Star of Bethlehem, with its upturned point symbolizing Spirit in charge of the four lower elements.

Manuel went on to explain how the rose symbolized desire, an aspect of Humanity in need of further cultivation. The most beautiful roses were always cultivated roses, grown with love and care. Intelligent pruning encouraged the production of the most magnificent flowers, and Rosalie needed to be careful of the thorns, another aspect of desire, for desires could sometimes bring pain as well as the beauty and fragrance symbolized by the flower. Though the thorns were a necessary part of the plant, a built-in protection system designed by Nature.

Wild shoots needed to be removed along with weaker stems so the plant could generate ample blossoms. Wild shoots usually grew from beneath the main root, robbing the plant—another symbol for Humanity—of strength derived from the soil, its source of nourishment. Wild shoots weakened the plant, as excessive or unnecessary activity sabotages the soul when it comes to productivity and expansion. Wild shoots represented untamed energy run amok, dissipated without purpose.

"How did you learn all of this?" Rosalie was amazed to discover that pruning a rosebush meant so much.

"Justin taught me. It's Ageless Wisdom passed on from generation to generation among the fairy folk. Plants are special beings to them. The flowers produce seeds for a new generation, regardless of what kind of plant it is. That's why flowers are so special. Flowers are vital to the reproduction of all plants anywhere in the universe."

Justin's ancestors had learned everything they knew from the Hierarchy of Light in the very beginning of the Dispensation of Time, millennia ago.

"Wild roses are nice," Manuel said as he handed her a fully bloomed pink rose, exquisite and perfect, "but there's nothing like the beauty of a cultivated rose."

Rosalie raised the flower to her nose, inhaling its sweet fragrance; then Manuel wrapped his arms around her, hugging her to him, breathing in the sweet fragrance of Rosalie. She felt good to him and she felt good to herself. She felt loved. That was important. Manuel rubbed his face in her soft, dark hair, enjoying the scent of her, his festival of roses. She was as delicate as any flower and just as beautiful. And her stems weren't bad either.

Manuel thought about the strength in Rosalie, strength worthy of cultivation. But he was also aware of the thorns, the rough spots in her character in need of careful handling. Though Manuel was not afraid of the thorns. He never wore gloves while pruning roses. Sometimes he pricked his fingers and they bled a little, but he would take his chances, for the blossoms were fragrant and beautiful, a fitting prize for small pain.

"Prune well, princess," he told her, kissing her nose. "And one day you shall surely win the prize."

Rosalie studied him, then squared her shoulders and somewhat apprehensively approached a sprawling red rosebush. The blossoms were crimson, blood-red. One rose was fading beyond its glory. Without saying a word, Manuel handed her the pruning shears.

For a brief moment, she hesitated; then she found a strong five-leaf section of the stem and cut the flower free from the bush. She felt some sadness as she looked down at the fading rose in her hand. Her brief movement caused the petals to separate from the stamen and flutter to the grass—scattered red rose petals at her feet.

"Fret not, fair maiden," Manuel proclaimed as he playfully ruffled her hair. "Another blossom shall take its place, more glorious and beautiful than the last. For its strength is derived from the same stem and its nourishment from the same root. The bush will give birth to many new blossoms under your tender loving care. Just don't forget to water them wisely and well, not too much, not too little."

"Oh, Wise Counselor of the Rosebush," she playfully answered, "how will I know how much is too much or how much is too little?" She curtsied before him.

"By paying attention and using your head," he tapped her on top of her head. "And sometimes by making mistakes. Just remember, you'll always get another chance—always."

Manuel placed his arm around Rosalie's shoulders as she slipped her arm around his waist. They stood side by side, gazing at the beautiful rose garden before them. It had bloomed in magnificent splendor under Manuel's dedicated care. Now Rosalie would have her turn.

Upon hearing the faint haunting music of the carousel in the distance, Manuel's thoughts drifted back to his meeting with Marcella at first light. He tenderly hugged Rosalie, and in mutual unspoken assent they began walking toward the lake.

Manuel finally broke the silence by saying, "My younger sister, Rosa, has married a Greek. Alexander Apollonius."

"That's a mouthful," Rosalie replied, smiling.

"Yeah," Manuel said, laughing. "He's Greek Orthodox. He and Rosa eloped. Naturally, Mama wasn't too happy about that. He's a musician. Alexander plays classical violin."

"That's great. He can play her love songs, beautiful love songs," Rosalie said with a sigh, watching the waves lap against the shore. There was a large sailboat out on the water. The breeze seemed stronger than on most days.

"Yeah, love songs would be good," Manuel thoughtfully replied. "Alex plays for the New York Philharmonic. Not bad, huh—the Sierras with a long-haired musician in the family?"

"That's nice, Manuel. Really nice."

Manuel was in a pensive mood when he said, "I think Mama should be proud and grateful for the class he brings to the family. No one else in the family has ever had that kind of talent. Just imagine, all their kids could be musical. It would be great having cousins like that."

He avoided looking at her when he reached down to pick up a rock and tossed it out into the lake. Together they watched concentric circles spread out larger and larger, creating small waves that eventually disappeared from view. Yet, beneath the surface the movement continued on and on across the lake, affecting myriad beings and forms.

"Rosa Apollonius," he said aloud, amused. "Is that a mouthful or what?"

Together they laughed, then hugged each other. She felt so good to him, his Rosalie, so warm and comforting to his touch. To her, he felt strong and protective, loving and gentle. They kissed long and sweet, hoping it would last forever, that the moment would not pass—but it did.

Waves splashed against the shore, each one distinct, propelled by the same Source and returning thereto. The surface of the lake was in continual motion yet constant within its boundaries, as the soul is constant, though the outward form may constantly change. Sunbeams danced on the surface of the water. On the far side of the lake misty clouds drifted above tall pines as a perfect rainbow formed, heralding the passing of a cloudburst. Gregoria should be pleased that his undines had painted the sky so beautifully. The rainbow promised sunshine—the coming of the Light.

The music of the carousel could now be heard. It grew louder, more enchanting, more distinct as they continued walking along without speaking as they had in the forest, hand in hand, arm in arm, and sometimes without even touching, except in thought. Their hearts were in tune like the notes of the carousel, playing in sweet harmonics. It was a day of joy in the eternal sun.

"Are your other sisters and brothers married?" Rosalie was the one to break the silence.

"All except Carlos, my little brother. He's the handsome one. All the girls are mad about Carlos. All he has to do is wiggle his little finger and the girls come running. It's amazing." Manuel was shaking his head. "You know, he works out at the gym all the time building up big, bulging biceps and muscles. Mr. Wonderful, that's Carlos. He could end up as Mr. America."

"Good for him," Rosalie said. "But I've never been too crazy about big, hard muscles on a man." She made a face. "A nice body is fine, but no Tarzan for me, thank you very much." She smiled as she turned to face him. "I like your body just fine, at least the divine edition."

He smiled as he hugged her, then said, "Juan, my oldest brother, he married a widow. He adopted her three kids. In fact, he's already a grandfather. And Hector, he married a girl from Ecuador. They're expecting their third child. The family is growing and growing. Lots of kids, lots of husbands and wives. Most of them seem to be settling down." Manuel grew quiet, a bit uneasy. He stared off at the horizon. The rainbow was no longer in sight.

"How about Theresa, your baby sister?" Rosalie asked. "You know, the one with the goldfish?"

Manuel looked away when he said, "Theresa married an Italian last year, Antonio Valenti. Mama's happy she at least married a Catholic, except they never go to church. Theresa's the liberated one in my family. A liberated woman. She won't let Mama get away with playing the tyrant. Not with her. Not on your life."

"Good for Theresa! What does Antonio do?"

"He drives a cab," Manuel said, matter of fact. "But he's going to school. He's studying to be an engineer. He's smart, Antonio, and very ambitious. Besides that, he loves Theresa. He's good to her. They have a good relationship, a very solid relationship."

"That's great! I always thought she was your favorite."

He took a deep breath before saying, "Theresa's pregnant. She's praying for a son."

Rosalie suddenly stopped and turned to look at him. She noted the faraway look in his eyes as a strange gnawing sensation began to fill her entire being. "Do you think Theresa will be a good mother?" she deliberately asked as a chill rippled over her body.

"Probably," was Manuel's flat response as he tried for nonchalance. "You're right, you know, even though she never liked the names I gave her goldfish, she always was my favorite. She used to tell me about all her problems with her fifth-grade teacher, Mrs. Waring, and her girlfriend, Michelle. And even though Theresa is not a really strict Catholic, she still lights candles for me every year. For a while she lit them every day, every single day for months. She's going to night school, studying to be a psychologist. She's a determined woman, Theresa. She's going to get somewhere in that world. She'll help people. I know she will."

Directly in front of them was the grand carousel, motionless, soundless, a misty golden light within and all around it. On the platform right in front of them was a large crystal bench designed like a cloud with a brilliant rainbow shining above it—a rainbow tied with a large bow of light blue.

In silent mutual assent they stepped up onto the platform and sat down on the violet cushions on the crystal cloud beneath the radiant rainbow. It reminded Rosalie of Felicia and Gregoria and the water nymphs, of the special time they had all spent together on Manuel's mountain. Everything was so peaceful and serene. But Manuel was thinking about other things. He was remembering his meeting with Marcella at first light, his decision. He took in a quiet breath as he placed his arm around Rosalie. She instinctively nestled her head against his shoulder. In that instant their hearts were filled with unspeakable joy.

"Just think," Rosalie whispered, "if I hadn't fallen off that roof, we might never have met. Strange, isn't it?"

"Very strange," Manuel replied, an amused look on his face. "Sometimes terrible things lead to wonderful things and one thing leads to another. Suppose I wasn't crazy about roses? Then I never would have taken care of your rose garden."

Rosalie sat forward and turned to look at him, reaching up to touch his face. "And you wouldn't be interested in a festival of roses." Her lips waited to be kissed, her eyes filling with tears of love and adoration.

"I love you, Rosalie," he said, and he kissed her, sweetly, tenderly.

"I love you so, Manuel," she replied, brushing tears from her cheeks. "And the strangest part about it is—it's like I've always loved you and always will."

"Me too," he softly replied and again he kissed her lips with a multitude of tender kisses.

Ever so slowly, the carousel began to turn in clockwise motion, and the faint, haunting music began to play. Melodious, angelic harmonics accompanied their kisses and serenaded their love. Then they sat back to enjoy the ride. Her hand was gently resting in his as the hypnotic heavenly music played on.

❧

Then the carousel began turning faster and faster, picking up speed, and the music became louder and louder as the carousel spun around and around and around. It was then that they caught sight of the brass ring—the bright, shining, beckoning brass ring glittering in the morning light.

"I'll find you," Manuel told her, his tone determined, his jaw set, as he stared straight ahead. "No matter what happens, I know that I'll find you." Tears were welling up in his eyes.

Rosalie turned to him, a bewildered expression on her face. There was confusion in her eyes as she asked him, "What do you mean, Manuel? What do you mean, you'll find me?" She was searching his brown eyes for the answer.

He silently turned away, afraid to look at her. He was afraid to look into those loving, brown eyes, afraid that the depth of their love would make him change his mind.

"I'm here, Manuel," Rosalie insisted as an overwhelming sense of emptiness enveloped her—a sense of loss that was frightening. "I'm right here," she said. She was having trouble breathing. She took Manuel's face in her hands, trying to get him to look at her.

"Manuel," she was nearly shouting, her soul was demanding an explanation. "You have to tell me what you're talking about. What do you mean, Manuel? What do you mean when you say that you'll find me?"

He finally turned to look at her, tears coursing down his cheeks. He gathered her into his arms, holding on for all he was worth, as the carousel spun round and round and round, faster and faster.

"I love you, my festival of roses," he said, kissing her again and again. He looked into her bewildered, tear-filled eyes. "I love you and I'll find you. We'll build a life together, you and me. I promise. A good life, you'll see. We'll get married and raise a family. It will be great. You have to trust me, Rosalie. Marcella has made me a promise."

"But I don't understand," Rosalie began to weep. "I keep hearing about this Marcella and all she knows about my life, and I've never even met her." She tried to fight back the tears. "How can I trust her? I don't know her from Adam."

"You can trust me, princess," was the promise in his eyes as he smiled through his tears. "We'll meet on a carousel. It will be wild and crazy and romantic. You'll love it. I'll be an Aries." He felt so helpless and torn as the brass ring kept passing him by, flashing and beckoning in the light. Beckoning for him to reach up and out. He stared at the brass ring as it approached him again. Rosalie was watching him. He hesitated, turning back to her.

"It won't be long. It'll just be a drop in eternity," he assured her, taking her hands in his. "And you'll be married before you're twenty-five. I promise!"

He stood up, forcing a smile. Rosalie desperately shook her head. She was clutching his hands, tears streaming down her cheeks.

"It's too soon," she protested through her tears. "We've only had a moment, just a moment together here. It's too soon, Manuel. It's just too soon."

In that instant, he could not answer her for he was being pulled, magnetically drawn by an invisible force, propelled and driven toward the edge of the revolving platform. Rosalie helplessly held on to one of his hands with both of hers, unwillingly pulled along, pulled by a powerful, determined, invisible force.

Manuel now stood at the edge of the platform as it whirled in clockwise motion around and around, faster and faster. With his free hand he grasped the crystal pole to steady himself. Rosalie was still desperately clinging to his other hand.

"I can't let you go." The tears freely flowed. "I can't," she told him, her chest heaving in great sobs. She was trying to catch her breath.

"We have forever, princess," he said softly yet firmly, looking right into her eyes. From somewhere deep within he had found his strength. He was strong, very strong. He knew what he had to do. There was nothing Rosalie could say or do to dissuade him. He had made a promise—to Marcella, to the Hierarchy, to Theresa, to himself. He had a job to do on earth. One day she would understand, and together they would accomplish many things. Only time would tell the rest of their story, a story they had yet to begin anew.

Rosalie sensed the sudden change in him—the determination, the conviction emanating from his soul. She understood a semblance of the truth in his unspoken words, his thoughts. She had no choice, none at all. Slowly she released his hand. It was Time. Time was beckoning. Time would win. She would have to trust him. She had no choice but to believe his promise.

"How will I know you?" she asked, trying to control the tears, trying to be brave for his sake. "How will I find you?"

"My name will be Nicholas," he told her, "Nicholas Valenti." He was trying to contain his tears. He half-smiled and cried out, "Don't you dare marry another guy!"

Coming towards him, sparkling and shining was the brass ring, reflecting tiny beams of blinding light. He cast one last glance at Rosalie, who stood breathlessly watching, her heart wildly beating to the crescendoing music that beckoned him to Life, as Manuel reached up and caught the brass ring. In a flash of dazzling, brilliant, white light that immediately reflected all the colors of the rainbow, he was gone. Vanished. Out of sight.

For a moment Rosalie just stood there, unable to move. She stared at the empty space where he had been. She was trying to cope with the reality of the moment, the drama they had just enacted. One instant he was there. The next he was gone out of sight, out of reach, out of touch. He had gone to a totally different dimension.

As the carousel slowly came to a stop, in the distance the protesting cry of a newborn baby was heard, wailing for all he was worth. He was letting the world know his discomfort and annoyance at having been extracted from the love and warmth and security of another, finer dimension. Rosalie now understood why newborn babies cry.

She took a deep breath and walked to the place where Manuel had stood only moments before. Gingerly she reached up, lightly touching the pole where his hand had been. Somewhat in a daze she looked up at the new brass ring now in place, the shining brass ring that was beckoning, tantalizing, sparkling in the light. She started to reach up, stopping just short of it, then withdrew her hand. It wasn't Time. Time wasn't calling her. Rosalie was not ready just yet.

With great reluctance, she stepped down from the platform and stood there alone. Silent tears were streaming down her face. She took a deep breath and sighed, bravely brushing away the tears.

"I'll find you, Nicholas Valenti," she promised, her voice just above a whisper but her tone determined. "I'll prune the roses just the way you taught me, and when we have a home of our own, we'll have a rose garden and we'll prune the roses together. We'll have beautiful roses, lots and lots of them in every possible color and variety of bloom."

Her eyes filled and overflowed with tears as she looked up at the carousel with its magnificent crystal unicorn, winged lion, and Pegasus draped with garlands of red roses. The brass ring was still there in sight, glittering in the light.

"I'll find you, Nicholas!" she shouted at the sun shining up in the heavens. "With God's help, I will find you someday!" ✾

Chapter Eighteen

Each day in eternity Rosalie took time to prune the roses. She planted strawberries in the empty cultivated corner in the garden, twelve plants. She carefully tended her garden with love, especially the rose garden. She was watering it, learning how much was enough and how much was too little.

Sometimes she visited with Aunt Beatrice in Seaside. Together they took mineral baths and long walks along the beach, watching the waves crash on the shore. They spoke of former days and times together on earth. The two of them shared many memories, most of them happy.

Due to a recent coronary, Uncle Irving was on a strict diet. His cholesterol was too high and so was his blood pressure. He needed to be more careful. Uncle Irving was trying. But he was a stubborn man.

Eternity was marking time. Yet without Manuel, for Rosalie it was an eternity. Rosalie was learning to paint with oils. It was something she had always wanted to do. On many days she painted ethereal, whimsical portraits of Aleatha and Felicia, her favorite undines. Rosalie was showing promise, although her talent was still in need of refinement. At least she was developing her gift.

There were times when she visited Manuel's mountaintop with Timothy, Irving, and Penny. But it was not the same without Manuel. The undines and elves tried to cheer her. They wanted to make her happy with their music and games. She enjoyed watching them leap from plant to tree in sparkling streaks of light. The air sylphs and salamanders put on fantastic fireworks displays that lit up the night sky. They were grander than anything Rosalie had ever seen on earth. For brief moments her emptiness was filled—but only for moments.

Lately, she had heard talk that Marcella was preparing festivities for the Summer Solstice. The festival was to take place in a large open meadow with a vast array of glorious plants and flowers. There was to be feasting, singing, and dancing all day long in the light of the sun that continued well into the night, beneath the glowing full moon and radiant stars above in the heavens. A special guest had promised to make an appearance, someone higher up in the Hierarchy of Light. Timothy was anticipating the event with some excitement. But in her dispassionate state of melancholy, Rosalie was filled with longing and yearning. She couldn't help but wonder just how long it would be before she could be reunited with her beloved Manuel—now known as Nicholas.

"How long has it been?" she inquired of Timothy.

"Two years in earth's time."

"Two years?" was Rosalie's complaint. "That's forever."

Timothy affectionately took her hand, trying to give what comfort he could. Penny and Irving were happily swimming in the lake. Rosalie had been working at her large easel, with an even larger canvas on it, near the water's edge. She was painting a landscape of the lake with the tall towering trees in the distance. Most of the time now she avoided the carousel. Her memory of her last ride with Manuel was still far too painful.

"Tomorrow is the Summer Solstice," Timothy announced in an attempt to lighten her mood. "And you will finally meet Marcella. It's a very important day for you."

"It seems like I've waited forever to meet the lady of mystery," she quietly responded. "You know that she prom-

❧

ised Manuel that we'll be together on earth, that we'll be married. I feel it's time for her to make that same promise to me." She stared off into space. "The least she should do is promise that we'll be together again sometime soon."

"That is up to you and Marcella, my dear girl," Timothy confessed. "It is entirely out of my hands."

Rosalie knew that Timothy would help her in any way he could. The bond between them had grown close and meaningful. Rosalie loved Timothy like a member of her own family. It was just that she missed Manuel so very much. Regardless of how hard she tried, she simply could not stop thinking about him. She thought about him all the time, everyday. Everything around her reminded her of Manuel, even Timothy.

"I wish there were some way we could make tomorrow today," she remarked half in jest, but when she began to really think about it she decided to ask, "Is there a way, Timothy? Is there any way to make tomorrow today?"

Timothy began to think about it, really think about it. It seemed to him in all probability that such a thing was highly possible. After all, they did exist in the Eternal Now. There was certainly nothing either of them could lose by trying.

"Come, lass," he said with a twinkle in his eyes, "take my hands and we'll see if we can make a wee demonstration of the luck of the Irish."

Heaven had been so full of miracles that one more would not surprise Rosalie, so she placed her hands in Timothy's. She knew she could trust him with all her heart.

"Now close your eyes," he told her, "and in your mind's eye see alabaster pillars gleaming in the sunlight—great, grand pillars of white marble twenty feet high. Pillars hand-carved by Greek master craftsmen. Can you see them?"

"I'm working on it." Rosalie's eyes were closed tight. She was concentrating for all she was worth, squinting, frowning. Nothing seemed to be happening.

"Perhaps if you don't try quite so hard," Timothy patiently advised. "Relax your mind, lass. Let it go. The sky is blue and there are wispy clouds out on the horizon. And in the distance you can hear the sound of the ever-restless sea crashing time and again against the craggy shore. There's a scent of salt in the air. And all around you can see rich green grass rolling on and on and on, as far as the eye can see. You can see every type of flower and plant the mind can even imagine, and then some." He was really getting into it.

"The sun is shining, of course. And the temperature, well, it's pleasant like here in Lakeside, not too hot and not too cold. It's just right. And if you listen closely now you can hear the musicians tuning up their harps and their lutes and their flutes, and the music they are playing is heavenly music, a touch Greek, since that's the way Marcella likes it. None of us object, of course, because it's grand and quaint and charming."

"I can see the pillars!" Rosalie announced in a rush of excitement. She had stopped squinting. A soft smile formed on her face. She was beginning to tune in on the scene that Timothy was describing.

"There are long banquet tables filled with fruit and nuts and all the good and succulent things grown upon the earth," Timothy went on, presenting a vivid description of the Solstice event.

"And roast lamb?" Rosalie licked her lips.

"Good heavens, no!" was his immediate response. His energy field malfunctioned only slightly. "We eat no creatures here, lass. Not at the festival of the Summer Solstice. Here we celebrate the Light on a much higher and grander frequency."

"I guess I can settle for fruit and nuts," Rosalie replied, a touch disappointed. "But I still like roast lamb, regardless of the frequency."

Timothy crossed himself, an old habit. Not that he hadn't occasionally enjoyed a roast lamb on earth at times himself, but certainly not at Marcella's celebration of the Solstice. Poor lambs, he thought. Here the creatures were free to frolic in the meadows along with everyone else.

"I can smell the salt air," she said as she took in a deep breath. "And I can see the clouds in the sky."

"And everywhere you look there are beautiful people merrily running about," he continued. "Some are dancing. Some are singing. Others are just being friendly. And everyone is dressed in the elegant fashions of ancient Greece, partly because it's the Solstice and partly because it's so comfortable and allows such free movement."

"And because it's so pretty," she remarked with a smile. "So flowing and beautiful."

Now she could hear the music, the harps and lutes and the impish flutes. She could hear the lyrical voices of the singers, and she could see the dancers gliding gracefully across the grass, sweeping and flowing in time with the beautiful music.

Just like a little girl preparing for a wonderful surprise, Rosalie partially opened one eye. The scene before her remained exactly the same as it had been in her mind. They were standing on Marcella's island. In the distance the mighty marble temple glistened upon a knoll with sunlight reflecting dancing beams of light, sparkling and resplendent. It was more than lovely. It was grand.

"Holy shit!" Rosalie exclaimed.

Timothy immediately opened his eyes. It was not the reaction he had hoped for, but it was Rosalie. All things considered, his energy field took it rather well.

Rosalie could not believe her eyes. Never before had she seen so many beautiful people gathered in one place. All the men looked strong and handsome, with bodies like Greek gods. They wore bright, colorful tunics, some in rainbow hues. It was a dazzling sight. The women all looked so elegant, winsome, and lovely in their long, beautiful gowns. Rosalie wished that she had changed her clothes for the occasion.

"But you have," Timothy told her, beaming with pleasure. "Just look at yourself, lass!"

When Rosalie looked down she discovered that she was wearing a pale yellow gown of soft organza, gathered about her waist with a gold sash, all very Greek. She responded with a girlish giggle.

"Being dead is such fun. It's like being in a fairy tale and discovering that you're a princess."

"Ah, but you are a princess," a lyrical voice proclaimed, a voice that generated warmth throughout Rosalie's entire being.

It was the voice of Marcella who now stood before her in a flowing white gown. Around her shoulders was a cape of bright golden yellow to symbolize the Sun's radiance. She looked luminous. Upon her head was a splendid sunburst crown of purest gold. The twelve points of the crown were adorned with different precious stones to represent the mighty constellations, the eternally rotating vastness of the zodiac in the heavens.

Without being introduced Rosalie knew that this was Marcella. Like everyone else, Rosalie, too, became awestruck by her exquisite beauty—not just her outward appearance but the inner radiance of pristine purity that glowed from within her. Rosalie could feel the love emanating from the heart of Marcella touch her own heart, her own core. It affected her like wondrous music that makes one want to cry. For a moment, Rosalie could not find her voice. She was too dazzled by the light coming from the celestial beings now standing before her.

Rosalie slowly regained her composure. It was then she became more fully aware of the two men standing on either side of Marcella. The man on her right appeared to be in his mid-thirties. He was tall and broad-shouldered. He looked strong and powerful, very powerful. His curly blond hair was short, his chiseled face handsome, with a deep cleft in his chin. His eyes reminded her of bright blue sapphires, with a star twinkling in each one. He easily possessed the magnificence of a Greek god. An amused, paternal expression formed on his face. Naturally, he was reading her mind.

"I am Matthias," the man informed her, his voice deep, melodious. "Welcome to the festival of the Summer Solstice."

Rosalie couldn't answer him. Timothy was spellbound. Together they stared in silence.

Matthias was a radiant soul—even transcendent. Marcella was exactly the same. In beholding them, all Rosalie could think of was love. Pure, unadulterated Divine Love—a wonder to behold.

The other man standing beside Marcella appeared younger, except that he, too, was shining and resplendent. He reminded Rosalie of impressions she had of Alexander the Great. His appearance was classical though nearly transparent. The contour of his face was perfectly symmetrical—strong, beautiful, angelic even. That was it! He looked just like an angel. He was tall, very tall. And there was something about his eyes that looked right into her soul. It was unnerving, yet made her feel somehow secure. He reminded her of someone she could count on. Someone who would be there for her whenever she needed him. He looked like a warrior, so virile. His reddish-blond hair was long and wild, not the short military style of Matthias. Rosalie could not shake off the feeling that there was something familiar about this guy—something very familiar.

"Don't I know you from somewhere?" she blurted out.

"We felt it was time for you to meet Michael," Marcella told her. "You are in his charge."

"I am?" Rosalie gulped. No question, this guy was gorgeous. "Hello, Michael," she finally managed, feeling suddenly shy.

Michael had always been one of her favorite names. When she was a little girl, Rosalie had had an imaginary friend she called Michael whom she would talk to when there wasn't anybody else around. When she was four she tried to introduce him to her mother. Mama just said that she had an overactive imagination, so she never tried to introduce Michael to anyone again. Why bother?

Michael was watching her closely. He nodded a radiant smile, then disappeared—vanished into thin air just like that!

Rosalie blinked and looked around everywhere. He was gone, nowhere in sight. "Was it something I said? Did I do something wrong?" she asked.

With a loving expression on her face Marcella slipped her arm around Rosalie's waist to lead her toward the banquet tables "Michael is your guardian angel," Marcella explained.

Rosalie shivered from head to toe, goose bumps all over her. "Guardian angel?"

"That he is," Timothy chimed in, walking along with Matthias. He was so pleased to have finally met Marcella's soulmate.

"That was my guardian angel?" Rosalie was a bit shaken, and still trying to figure out where he'd gone. "So where did he go? What kind of a guardian is that, for Chris...," she caught herself. "What I mean is, how can he guard me when he isn't even around?"

"He's around," Matthias assured her. "Angels can be a bit shy when it comes to mortals. But rest assured, Michael is one of the best. He is delighted to have you in his charge, and is pleased with your progress."

"For you see, Rosalie," Marcella said, "Michael has been looking after you forever. Up until now you were not ready to meet him in this dimension. But we decided that the time was right."

"You mean that gorgeous guy, I mean, angel, has been looking after me, just me, all this time?" She was amazed.

"Just you," Matthias said, smiling.

"I think I'm in love," was her girlish reply.

"You are love," Marcella acknowledged, hugging her. "Michael finds you an absolute delight. He shall continue to guard you wisely and well."

✿

"He shall continue to have his hands full, too," Timothy added with a grin.

"All guardian angels do, my dear Timothy," Marcella chided, then laughed. "You haven't always made Nathaniel's task an easy one."

"I don't suppose so," Timothy stood corrected. It was always a simple task for Marcella to make him feel like a child.

"How about Manuel?" Rosalie asked. "Does he have a guardian angel, too? I'd feel a lot better knowing there was someone there looking after him."

"Everyone has a guardian angel," Marcella explained. "Manuel's guardian is Muriel."

"Is that a he or a she angel?" Rosalie inquired. All she needed at that point was to find out that some gorgeous female angel was looking after Manuel.

"Angels are neither male nor female," Matthias told her. "They're androgynous."

"What does that mean?" was her response.

"Think of them as sexless," Marcella chimed in. "It will ease your mind."

It wasn't all that easy for Rosalie to think of Michael as sexless. Michael was magnificent, a really sexy-looking angel, especially with his light-blue piercing eyes. She hoped Muriel wasn't too beautiful. But as fate would have it, Rosalie doubted that there were any shabby-looking angels around. From a human perspective, she surmised that all angels had to be tens.

"If Manuel has a guardian angel, how come I never saw...*it*? I mean, I saw undines and elves and all the nature spirits."

"It is rare to glimpse the guardian of another, even in this dimension," Marcella admitted. "Most mortals never even see their own angelic protectors. You may rest assured, dear Rosalie, that your Manuel, or shall we say Nicholas, is very well looked after and very well protected."

"Muriel has been with his soul as long as Michael has been with yours," Matthias added. "Muriel serves him now just as Michael will be serving you during your forthcoming life incarnate."

"And as Nathaniel will be serving you, dear Timothy," Marcella informed him in the midst of sending Timothy a mini-love jolt of bright pink light.

"The two of you have grown so close here," Matthias now addressed them both. "You should be happy in the same family. We will expect glowing reports from earth."

Rosalie and Timothy looked at one another in amazement, although there had been times when they had wished or wanted it so.

"I'll be your older sister," Rosalie announced. Somehow she just knew without being told. "Just you wait, Timothy O'Toole, I'll boss you around and make you wait on me hand and foot. Just you wait!"

"Now just a minute here," Timothy objected, squaring his shoulders, but just one glance from Marcella confirmed the order of descent. So the time was now approaching for his return to earth. A cold shiver ran up and down Timothy's spine. It was true that he would live in America, a country he had heard so many grand and interesting stories about. Many of his relatives from Ireland had migrated there a very long time ago. Perhaps he would run into a few of them. Now wouldn't that be interesting?

"Well, just you remember," Timothy informed Rosalie, "Little brothers do grow up and they usually end up far taller and stronger than any of their sisters, so just keep that in mind. Please do!"

Rosalie was delighted. Just the thought of having Timothy return to earth with her was a gift from God. During her last life she had often wished that she had a brother.

Marcella understood Rosalie's pleasure and sent a love wave to her core. It was a warm, tender, maternal kind of love, Love Divine, not the type of love she had come to know with Manuel. It was at that moment that Rosalie knew there was nothing to equal the love that awaited her—neither on earth nor in heaven. It was then that Rosalie remembered she needed to ask Marcella a very important question. Before she could even form the words, Marcella began to speak.

"You will meet Nicholas Valenti on a carousel in the year 2000 as accounted in earth time. I will not reveal where or exactly how it will happen, but I am promising you that it will take place. The meeting will be a fundamental part of your destiny. I will not deprive you of the joy of discovery that comes with living on earth, for your life would be quite dull without at least a few thousand surprises."

"Some I could do without," Rosalie admitted. "Like falling off a roof after being bombed by a defective crow."

Marcella and Matthias exchanged amused smiles, deep understanding in their eyes.

"We'll make sure that doesn't happen again," Matthias assured her.

"Thank God! Once was enough."

Rosalie turned to Timothy, who was smiling at her, true affection in his eyes, and said, "Life is so strange, Timothy!" Then she gave him a big hug.

"That it is," Timothy agreed, hugging her back.

"God knows," Marcella added.

"But wonderful!" Matthias threw in. Then Matthias placed his arm around Marcella's waist, pulling her to him. There was so much love between them, total admiration and respect. It was something miraculous to behold. It was love based on mutual trust and a rare level of understanding, love rarely seen.

In a state of reverence and wonder, Rosalie and Timothy watched as Marcella and Matthias walked off to mingle with other souls in need of their loving attention.

Then Rosalie saw a basket filled with crisp red apples. She picked one out and handed it to Timothy. "Try it, it's our kind of apple." She took another for herself.

They each took a bite, chewed and swallowed. The apples were crisp, not mushy. Rosalie was right. It was their kind of apple.

"Will we remember any of this?" Rosalie wistfully asked, as they surveyed the pageantry before them.

"Perhaps, although I've been told that remembering is a gift to be earned by the worthy," Timothy confided. "I don't know if it would do us any good to remember all of this. It might be easier in that dimension if we didn't."

"I think I know what you mean. It might just make us homesick."

"Souls often are, you know," he acknowledged. "It's the vague recollection of freedom from earthly flesh that keeps calling us back and sending us on until we evolve to the place where we can become like Marcella and Matthias. Look at them, Rosalie. Look at them now."

Marcella and Matthias had begun to dance. Their movements were as joyful and graceful as those of the finest ballet dancers, yet far exceeding even the best. They were superb. They were dancing the dance of Love, the dance of Being, the dance of expanding and growing into something far greater and finer, even God-like. Marcella and Matthias were dancing the Dance of Life. ✹

Chapter Nineteen

The next morning in eternity Rosalie awoke in a state of expectancy. There was a sense of excitement in the air. After enjoying a luxurious stretch against the slippery softness of her satin sheets, she sat up in bed. The air smelled sweeter and fresher than on most days. Everything around her had a special clarity, an extraordinary sharpness. She felt very much alive. A bluebird perched on the railing outside her bedroom window sang a song that welcomed the day. Rosalie stood up and stretched. Dear Irving was still snoozing, curled up in a ball in the corner of her room.

Memories of the Solstice festival were pouring through her mind. Marcella and Matthias stood out with the greatest clarity—two magnificent souls, loving and devoted to each other and to all souls assigned to their keeping. Divine love waves rippled through her as Rosalie held their images in her mind, an exercise capable of enhancing her evolution. For deep within her core Rosalie was beginning to understand the unity of life, the divine purpose of Love. Thoughts of love reminded her of Manuel, of David and Honey and Timothy, although the love she felt in her heart for Manuel seemed beyond the pale of the kind of earthly love she remembered. It was at that moment the delightful music of the carousel filled the morning air, renewing her anticipation, urging her to meet the day.

Timothy was in the kitchen with strawberry tea, biscuits, and jam on a tray. "I thought we might enjoy breakfast in the garden," he announced. "The roses are particularly lovely today."

Out in the garden they drank tea and ate biscuits with strawberry jam, a special gift from Aunt Beatrice.

Aunt Beatrice had been busy lately, learning new ways to cook and preserve all kinds of food. She was also busy making new friends, having recently been appointed to the welcoming committee in Seaside. Aunt Beatrice truly enjoyed meeting the new arrivals. Face it, Aunt Beatrice had a special knack for making souls feel right at home in any dimension.

It was true that the roses were especially lovely that day, much more magnificent than on any other day. Rosalie's meticulous pruning and loving care had ensured the new growth that would produce large fragrant blossoms, a few in transcendent shades, with each flower a wonder. The roses always reminded Rosalie of how she had first met Manuel in the garden. In fact, everything that morning was making her remember.

She remembered her arrival in Lakeside, and she remembered that first morning when she saw Manuel standing in the middle of the lawn surrounded by sunbeams, butterflies, and roses. She remembered how confidently he handled the roses, the tenderness and love he felt for all plants. But mostly, she remembered his soft brown eyes, his shining black hair, his glowing, golden skin, and the warmth of his embrace. How deeply Manuel had loved the roses. How deeply he had come to love her, his Rosalie—his festival of roses.

"How will we know each other when we meet?" she felt a sudden desperate need to ask.

"You'll know," Timothy assured her. "Your shared experiences and feelings are indelibly imprinted in the substance of your souls. In the beginning you may not totally understand the extraordinary feelings that come over you. That could take time. But you will know, my dear. Those who love always know."

Rosalie watched dear Irving chase a butterfly across the lawn. The air sylph riding upon the butterfly's back was giving Irving a run for his money. It made her smile to see it, though in another part of her being a deep sadness was beginning to well up.

Rosalie quietly surveyed the beauty all around her, the special beauty she had come to take for granted. She loved her mini-Tara. Her home in that dimension had provided her with much happiness and comfort. She remembered seeing Clark Gable and Carole Lombard walking beside the lake and wondered why they were still here when she was going back so soon. Then her consciousness became filled with the image of Manuel. She just had to see him again, touch him again, listen to him again, and love him again. Their destinies were intertwined and interwoven.

During their last lifetimes upon the earth each of them had died young in order that they might be reunited here on the other side. That meeting was important to their separate evolution as well as to their mutual destiny. And now destiny was drawing her back to earth—back to Manuel, to Nicholas. It was time to continue, time to go on. It was time to get on with the Plan.

"Different souls have different needs and different destinies," Timothy explained. "Some souls stay here a good deal longer and some go on to higher planes. Others feel the need to go back to get on with their special tasks. That is where you fit in."

Rosalie felt the need to turn and look at the waterfall at the deep end of the pool. She briefly glimpsed two water nymphs tumble in to take a swim and play. The joyful sight instantly took away her sense of sadness—the sadness she had carried since being separated from Manuel, and the sadness that had begun to envelop her now, due to her imminent departure from all she had come to know and love in this beautiful, extraordinary dimension. It was a dimension filled with joy and love, for life on earth for her had never before been a rose garden.

"You'll be better equipped this time," Timothy insisted.

"As long as I don't get David's nose." She cringed at the very thought. "Wouldn't that be something? Bad karma, I'd say."

"Please don't give it your attention," Timothy admonished. "You must begin thinking about the kind of nose you want right this minute."

Rosalie closed her eyes and started concentrating for all she was worth. She could only come up with an image of Honey's nose, which she found acceptable. She decided to settle, though she certainly hoped to keep the same skin tones she'd had during her last life. She had never been at all crazy about freckles, so she tried not to think about them. She understood the principle, but all the same, she kept on seeing Honey's freckled face.

"I think it is time for us to take a walk, lass," Timothy urged, noting that the carousel music had started playing just a bit louder, a bit stronger, beckoning for them to come and take a ride.

Rosalie reluctantly stood up and turned to him, a bittersweet smile on her face. Neither said a word. They simply started walking toward the lake, carefully weighing each step along the way.

"I'm going to miss traveling at the speed of thought," Rosalie admitted. "I haven't done it all that much, but...it's really something."

"That it is," Timothy nodded agreement.

"Life is so much easier here," Rosalie sighed. "There aren't any wars or sickness. Nobody can kill anybody. There aren't even any muggers."

"No muggers at all," Timothy agreed.

"Why can't life be like this on earth?" She was feeling distress. "Why do people on earth have to hurt each other all the time? It's so stupid."

"Because they have yet to learn that they are truly simply hurting themselves. They are all setting themselves up, my dear. They have to learn how to love, really love. Learning to love can take lifetimes. Many lifetimes, I fear." Timothy became quiet. His tasks here had taught him a great deal about love. He hoped he too would remember when it came time for him to return to earth. It wouldn't be long now, not long at all.

"I'll try to be a good sister," Rosalie promised, surprised at being able to pick up his thoughts.

"And I a good brother," he replied, his voice taking on a slight tremor. There were tears in his eyes. He would miss her, of course, and the thought of returning to earth in an entirely new set of circumstances made him a bit apprehensive. A creative Jewish father and an intuitive Scotch-Irish mother should prove an interesting way to settle a few of his karmic debts, though he was not allowed to see that far ahead for himself, of course. Only those higher up could do that, and there was talk that even they didn't have all the answers.

The carousel now came into view. The crystal unicorn and winged Pegasus and all the other mythical creatures were bedecked with garlands of bright pink roses. The sight was magical, charming; yet Rosalie and Timothy turned to one another with tears streaming down their cheeks. Their hearts and souls were filled with sadness and joy mixed with love. Their bond had been strengthened in that dimension to more securely interweave their destinies in the Tapestry of Time.

"I'll miss you, Rosalie," Timothy admitted without embarrassment, freely brushing tears from his cheeks as Rosalie kissed each one.

"Not for long, Timothy," she assured him, and in that instant her spirits lifted. "We know we'll be together again. We're sure of it. And I'll help take good care of you, I promise. You've been away from earth much longer than I have, and you've never lived in California. It's not so bad, really. They'll probably take us to Disneyland. You'll love it. It's the nearest thing we have to some of this."

Together they stepped up onto the platform. For a brief moment Timothy wanted to disappear. He hated farewells in general, and this one in particular. Yet he knew it would put a bad mark on his record, so he stayed, even though carousels usually made him dizzy.

Rosalie helped him up onto Pegasus, all draped with roses. That was when it dawned on her that they would be the generation of the future, the generation of an entire new century, a new millennium! All kinds of exciting new inventions and discoveries would be made while they were together on earth, discoveries that would serve evolution—discoveries for all humanity. Together they would share in the progress of a new beginning of a new Millennium of Time. The prospects were exhilarating.

"I think we should tell them what it's like here, Timothy. They need to know. I want you to try to remember."

Timothy felt as though he was caught up in a dream. He loved Pegasus with his wings spread wide. Pegasus reminded him of the stories from the distant past, heroic stories. Things had changed a great deal since Timothy had last been on earth. That would make life exciting, interesting, downright fascinating, in fact. After all, most Americans he had met in that dimension were not a bad lot, though he had found that was true of most souls once you got to know them. He became excited by the fact that he was about to embark on an entirely new adventure. Then the carousel slowly began to turn in a clockwise motion. The music began playing softly at first, but as the carousel turned faster, the music became louder, enchanting, entrancing, exciting yet soothing, all at the same time.

❋

Rosalie was standing next to Timothy as he sat astride mighty Pegasus. Her expression became quite serious as she began to plead, "You must promise me you will try to remember, Timothy. I promise that I will try. I'll let them know there is no death. That it's all just a dream. Promise me, Timothy. Please promise me that you'll try!"

"I promise," he finally relented, not altogether sure he would be able to keep his part of the bargain.

That was when Michael appeared, wearing a flowing violet robe with a gold and blue sash. His reddish-blond hair gleamed in the morning light. His penetrating blue eyes sparkled like the stars in the heavens. He was majestic, mighty, a magnificent angel—sexless or whatever.

"You are so beautiful, Michael," she couldn't help telling him.

He flashed her a radiant smile while remaining silent. It was plain to see even angels could enjoy a compliment.

"Please keep her off of roofs," Timothy beseeched him.

Michael nodded in sympathy to his request. There was, however, only so much an angel could do. He hoped she would pay better attention to her intuition this time around. He had a fine reputation as guardian angels go. The roof could not have been avoided. Hopefully, this time she would accept his protection instead of ignoring it, something that happens with so many mortals. It seemed to Michael that too many souls acted as though their guardian angels weren't even around. And yet, luckily for them, they always were.

"He'll always be with you," Timothy said of Michael. "He'll watch over you your whole life through, and it will be a long and good life, Rosalie, a very good life indeed."

"You will help to make it so, Timothy. I know you will."

That was when Rosalie saw the brass ring, shining and reflecting in the morning light, tantalizing her with its radiance, beckoning for her to reach up and grasp it. It was finally time for her to catch it and hold on tight.

Michael stood where Manuel had been, patiently waiting. He held out a strong arm and extended his open hand.

Rosalie took a deep breath. With Michael there, guarding her, she walked to the place where he stood. With her left hand she grasped the crystal rod, leaving her other hand free as the music grew deeper and louder, melodiously penetrating her being. The music was filling her head and heart with its sweet harmonics as the carousel gained greater momentum, circling faster and faster and faster. Timothy leaned forward as the tension began to mount.

He could see Michael at his station, guarding her, a great golden aura emanating from all around him, appearing as two mighty wings encircling them both. Again and again, the brass ring passed her by. Each time Rosalie hesitated. She was holding her breath the way she always did when she was unnerved or excited. Then the image of Manuel flashed fully before her inward vision. Now he was Nicholas Valenti. On a street in Brooklyn a small toddler was learning how to ride a tricycle. He was half-Italian and half-Puerto Rican. He had thick, curly, black hair, and big, brown eyes with long, sweeping lashes. His body was strong like his father's. He had his mother's independence, his mother's temper, his mother's courage and zest for life.

Young Nicholas loved to build things with blocks—forts and strange structures. He had quite an active imagination and a great sense of color. He often drew rainbows, beautiful, beautiful rainbows out of a multitude of colors. They were not ordinary rainbows at all. And he loved picking flowers for his mother, especially roses, even when the thorns pricked his small fingers. Mostly, Nicholas liked doing things for himself. He was bright, very smart. The family was very proud of young Nicky. He truly enjoyed giving and receiving hugs and kisses. He was a loving, joyful child, and something he liked best of all was riding the big carousel in the park.

On the carousel he always watched the little girls, all the little girls. He seemed to watch them very carefully, very closely. He was looking for someone, someone special. One day he knew in his heart that he would find her, one day on a carousel—when he became a man.

"Here I come, Nicholas Valenti!" she shouted out at the top of her voice. "Don't you dare forget that you promised to marry me before I'm twenty-five. Because if you forget, I'll never let you hear the end of it for as long as you live, which is going to be one hell of a long time!" She took a deep breath and caught the brass ring, holding on for dear life.

She began falling, falling, falling—falling and whirling into total darkness. The bright light of Lakeside faded out of sight, seemingly gone forever. It seemed as though she would never stop falling into the utter darkness surrounding her. Fear gripped her heart. She suddenly felt alone, and yet there was a slight fluttering of wings that seemed to surround her, to soften and break her fall.

Good old Michael, she remembered, I nearly forgot about you. She couldn't actually see him, but she knew that he was there protecting her, guarding her. Guardian angels never err as humans often can and do.

All at once she found herself in a long, dark tunnel. There was something pushing her, shoving her. It was so uncomfortable. Dying had been nothing like this. Good grief! Still she had this mild sensation of falling but nothing like before. That was when she began to hear voices, but she couldn't understand a thing they were saying.

At the end of the tunnel was a bright circle of light. She was beginning to feel dizzy from the whirling, the spinning, and the falling, when all of a sudden—she was out in the light.

All around there were bright lights glaring, sterile white walls, shining metal. A man and two women dressed in green were staring at her with probing, searching, questioning eyes. Then someone held her up in the air. It was a masked man. He turned her upside down. That did it. The only thing left to do was let out a loud, shrill, protesting cry.

"Congratulations, Mrs. Rosenberg. It's a girl!" the masked man announced, placing her on her mother's stomach while a nurse stood by ready to wrap her in something that was certainly not satin. No question, this was not heaven.

Touchdown, she thought to herself, and I can't even tell them I'm back. Are they ever in for a big surprise! ✳

Chapter Twenty

The success of David's book had provided the Rosenbergs with a comfortable three-bedroom home on a nice, quiet street without sidewalks in Encino. Nearly all of their neighbors cared enough to take good care of their yards. It was a definite improvement.

Honey had planted daisy bushes and geraniums in the backyard, where there was lots of sun. David had planted a peach tree on the south side of the house. It was doing nicely, and showed promise for the next season. The swimming pool was kidney-shaped with a slide, not really that big, but nice.

In the front yard there was a rose garden with eighteen bushes of various kinds and colors. Honey loved roses nearly as much as Rosalie had. It was late December. Only a few roses remained. January was pruning time, right after the Rose Parade in Pasadena. There would be lots of roses come spring. Chrysanthemums and geraniums still bloomed in the front yard—American Beauty geraniums, a bright fuchsia. The white, lavender, and pink mums were at the end of their cycle, a bit shabby. It was a chilly, rainy California December day.

On the way home from the hospital the streets were cheerily decorated for Christmas: Santa Claus with reindeer, large wreaths with red bows, and sparkling multicolored lights shining on houses and in windows. There were brightly bedecked trees with lights—some real, some artificial—glimmering and twinkling in the windows of homes and businesses. Many of the houses in Encino had multicolored or tiny white lights along the eaves or even outlining the roofs, as well as on trees and bushes. One house had plastic elves up on the roof, nothing at all like Justin and his friends. It was a feeble attempt at something she vaguely remembered, yet it was festive.

Rosalie was exasperated at finding herself in such a tiny body. But at the same time she was delighted that she could actually remember who she was and where she had been, and that she was actually back, even though there was no real way she could let them know. She had tried, of course, but she couldn't talk. All that came out of her mouth were squeaks and garbled baby sounds. It infuriated her, so naturally she cried. No wonder babies cry, she thought. She was beginning to understand a lot of things but it didn't help her a whole lot, so she cried some more. She thought she must have healthy lungs. She knew she had ten fingers and ten toes, except they were so tiny.

Honey was cradling her in loving arms on her first ride home from the hospital in the new car, humming to her, covering her forehead with tiny kisses, rubbing her soft motherly cheek against her baby face. It was nice. Really sweet. All she could do under the circumstances was gurgle and coo. What a predicament!

"Enjoy it," she heard a faint voice whisper. "You've earned it."

So Michael had a voice after all, a soothing, angelic sort of voice, really nice. She started to settle in. What else could she do under the circumstances?

"Sweet little Natalie," Honey cooed. "You're such a sweet baby, such a pretty, adorable child. Welcome to our world, Natalie. It's a wonderful world, a truly wonderful world. You'll see. We'll teach you all about it."

Natalie—Natalie Rosenberg. She guessed it wasn't such a bad name. They could hardly call her *Rosalie*. Honey might be a bit touchy on that score. Natalie had a nice sound to it, though it would take some getting used to.

David was steering the car into the driveway of their new home. He didn't really look that much different, a few more gray hairs. Other than that he looked pretty much the same. She had made a serious attempt to check out her nose with her hand but she couldn't quite make the move. She felt so clumsy and uncoordinated, so helpless. Her hands just wouldn't do anything that she wanted them to. Being a baby again had definite disadvantages that were proving frustrating, to say the least. She tried for her nose again. That was when they pulled the blanket down over her face, so she whimpered and fussed as they hurried with her up the walk in the lightly falling rain.

Inside the warm house, Kenny and Nancy were waiting to greet the new parents and baby girl just home from the hospital. Their own four kids were at home with a babysitter. After all, little Natalie was only three days old. Her cousins could meet her in a week or so. Rosalie had always thought they were a nice couple, really decent relatives. She had always been very fond of them. So Uncle Kenny and Aunt Nancy had come to see her. How nice, she thought, and how strange. She took a good hard look at Nancy, who had developed a somewhat matronly appearance. Nancy had put on a few pounds. After all, she had to be pushing forty. Nevertheless, she needed to go on a diet right after the holidays.

Then she saw the Christmas tree. It nearly touched the ceiling. On top was a bright, shining angel. It was beautiful. The tree was colorfully decorated in bright lights and shiny balls of red and green, silver, blue, and gold. Tiny hand-carved elves painted with bright colors perched on some branches. Clear glass fairies with pink wings were hanging from other parts of the tree. It made her feel right at home

213

and reminded her of the many wonders she had left on the other side.

Right beside the tree was a white wicker cradle. Little Natalie was placed in the cradle on her back so she could look all around. Now everyone could see her. Little Natalie. The new baby. They all began to bill and coo, to "ooohhh" and "aaahhh." If they could only see how silly they look, she thought at first, but after a just few minutes she really began to enjoy it. It was soothing, caring, loving, and quite nice.

"Hello, little Natalie," Uncle Kenny said, waving at her, all smiles. "You've just made me an uncle. How about that?"

"Natalie is such a pretty name, yes," Aunt Nancy cooed. Nancy always had been a cooer. "She's such a pretty baby, Honey. She's beautiful. Really beautiful."

People always say that, she thought. Even when the kid is ugly.

"You're a very pretty baby, Natalie. Yes, you are," Kenny was saying as he hovered above the cradle. His head looked bigger than she remembered it.

All she could do was try to look pleasant. She figured she wasn't managing a real smile, but she tried anyway. It felt okay to go along with their silly baby games. Besides, she was beginning to like being called Natalie. Just as long as nobody called her Nat.

That was when Daddy David lifted her out of the cradle and high up into the air in typical daddy fashion. He was smiling, really smiling.

"Hi, little Nat," he said to her, his eyes filled with pride. "How's Daddy's baby girl?"

Her only recourse at that point was to cry in angry baby protest. Nobody was going to call her Nat and get away with it. Naturally, Mommy came to her rescue immediately. Honey was cradling her little darling in loving arms, comforting her with tender kisses and motherly pats. She loved it.

"David," Honey chastised, "she's only a newborn, a tiny baby. You can't handle her like that until she's much older.

And please don't call her Nat. It's plain to see that she doesn't like it. We talked about that, remember? Her name is Natalie." Honey gave David a protective mother scowl before turning her full attention back to her precious newborn baby girl.

"Now, now, angel. Daddy didn't mean to frighten you. He doesn't understand, but he'll learn. You'll see. You just have to be patient with him. Sometimes daddies don't understand tiny babies in the very beginning, but he'll be a good daddy, just you wait and see. He'll be a wonderful father for you, my precious child, my sweet, sweet angel."

Oh brother, she thought to herself. Is this ever going to be interesting!

For a few moments, David looked downright dejected, but little Natalie didn't feel the least bit guilty about the situation. How else was she supposed to teach him a lesson?

That was the moment she caught sight of herself in the mirror over the fireplace mantelpiece. She had silky apricot hair, a peachy complexion, and her eyes looked bluish-green, almost the same color as the river that flowed near Halfway Point—the beautiful River of Life. She was delighted with her coloring. She tried smiling at herself in the mirror and discovered a tiny dimple in each of her cheeks. Not bad, she thought, not bad at all. She didn't look like anyone else she could even remember, even though she had always thought that all babies looked alike and rather ordinary. Maybe she was beautiful. There seemed to be some improvement from what she remembered of her old baby pictures.

Thank God she had not inherited David's nose. Her nose was tiny and turned up a touch, like lots of baby noses. She prayed time would be good to her. At least her nose wasn't anything like the nose in David's old baby pictures.

David was opening a gift from Kenny and Nancy while Honey placed her back in the cradle. Honey was gently rocking the cradle, back and forth, back and forth. Little Natalie was beginning to think it wasn't so bad being a baby. There were a few definite advantages, and she would grow up.

"How lovely!" Honey exclaimed, taking the gift from David. She held aloft a tiny carousel painted a variety of bright, shiny colors. It was musical, of course. She wound it up before placing it inside the cradle close to little Natalie.

The colorful carousel with its tiny animals in bright rainbow hues began to revolve, around and around. A familiar refrain serenaded her as the cradle continued to rock to and fro. *Rock-a-Bye Baby* was hardly original but not bad. In fact, it sounded quite nice.

She knew there was no way they could have possibly known what they had done, at least consciously, or was there? What they had done, of course, was remind her of the main reason she had come back—to find Nicholas. Nicholas Valenti. Somehow, somewhere, someday—on a carousel.

She thought maybe she might not always remember exactly why she had come back. In fact, she would probably soon forget, the way most souls do. But for now she remembered, and that dim memory in her soul would spur her on until she found him once again.

David was pouring champagne into crystal glasses so all of them could celebrate little Natalie's arrival, Honey's good health, and their new family unit. A very special delivery had arrived during a very special season of the year.

Secretly, David had wanted a son, but he wasn't totally disappointed that she was a girl. After all, she was healthy and whole. That was a blessing. And Honey had prayed hard for a daughter, a daughter to raise with love. Yet, David just knew that someday he would have a son, too. God had told him he would in a dream, and Honey had seen it in her teacup. And little Natalie absolutely knew that Daddy David's dream would soon come true, for she still dimly remembered Marcella's promise to her and Timothy at a special festival that celebrated the Light.

Briefly, little Natalie wondered what name they would give her little brother when he arrived. On that score she drew a total blank. As Marcella had said, life had to have at least a few surprises. She would find out when his soul arrived on earth. From the gleam in David's eye, she surmised it would not take a very long time.

As the cradle gradually came to rest, her wandering eyes caught sight of the Christmas tree lights reflected on the large screen of a new television set, faintly glowing circles of light dancing all about. The music from the little carousel was becoming fainter and slower, running down, down, down. She was beginning to feel drowsy, sleepy, peaceful, and contented. So that the last thoughts that went through her head before drifting off into a sweet, rather short, forgetful sleep were:

What do you know! I'll bet it's color. And I'll bet you anything they can get two and four. And something I can tell you for damn sure, I'm not climbing up on any roof under any circumstances whatsoever—and that's a promise!

It might not be heaven. But as far as she was concerned, it was perfect for a brand new beginning. ✳

Glossary of Names

Aleatha .... *Truth, unemotional awareness*
Alexander........................ *Helper of man, defender of man*
Antonio .... *Chiefly*
Apollonius .... *Belonging to Apollo, the Sun*
Beatrice .... *She who makes one happy*
Carol (Carole) .... *A melody, a song; pure*
Carlos.............................. *Happy, sociable, romantic*
Chili .... *Hot pepper*
Clark .... *Clergyman*
David .... *Beloved, alert, ingenious, honorable*
Felicia............................. *Happiness*
Gregoria .... *Vigilant, watchful*
Harriet .... *Ruler of the home; self-willed*
Hector .... *An anchor; steadfast*
Herbert .... *Illustrious by reason of an army*
Honey .... *A sweet, sticky material produced from the nectar of flowers*
Irving .... *Wielding, watchful*
Jonah .... *Lovable, fruitful, passionate*
Juan .... *Grace, mercy of the Lord*
Justin............................... *Just, true*
Kenneth .... *Self-seeking, handsome, brilliant*
Leonora .... *Like a lion*
Manuel (Emmanuel) ..... *God is with us; kindly, eloquent*

Marcella .... *Shining, brilliant*
Marcos .... *Shining, brilliant, polite*
Martin .... *Defender of the wronged*
Mary (Maria, Myrna) .... *Sea of bitterness; sorrow*
Matthias .... *Gift of God*
Michael .... *One who is like unto God*
Michelle .... *Meticulous, hard-working, patient*
Muriel .... *A bird; thoughtful, considerate*
Nancy .... *Graceful, merciful, unselfish*
Natalie .... *Christmas child; generous; peacemaker*
Nathaniel........................ *Given of God*
Nicholas .... *Victorious, popular, hard-working*
Penelope......................... *Faithful, loving, independent*
Rosa................................ *A rose; gracious, self-controlled*
Rosalie .... *Festival of roses; charming, faithful*
Sarah .... *Princess, noblewoman*
Scarlett .... *Flaming red*
Solomon .... *Peaceable, whole, complete*
Tara .... *To throw or to carry*
Theresa .... *Hard, severe, unyielding*
Timothy .... *Worshipping God*

About the Author

At the age of three months, Patricia McLaine was taken into a church in Kansas City, Kansas, by her mother to have her life dedicated to God. Clairvoyant since childhood, Patricia's visionary tales of fairies, angels, and the apparitions of departed relatives were dismissed by most relatives as the products of a highly active imagination. Her parents had met as missionaries and were deeply religious individuals. Young Patricia read the Bible from cover to cover when she was 14 years old and embarked on an in-depth study of comparative religion by the age of 25.

With such a background, it is not surprising that Patricia became a metaphysician by the age of 30. In addition to writing, she has taught and worked throughout the United States and various parts of the world as a tarot reader, astrologer, and clairvoyant for the past 33 years. At various times she has resided in Los Angeles, Northern Virginia, and Maine.

Her special talents have been featured in numerous books and articles, specifically the works of psychic researcher, Jess Stearn, *The Miracle Workers* and *Soulmates;* the autobiography of Susan Strasberg, *Bittersweet;* and the *Psychic Powers* volume of the popular Time-Life series, *Mysteries of the Unknown.*

Patricia now lives in Camden, Maine, where she does psychic consultations in person and by telephone for individuals all over the world. In addition, she is writing a beginners' book on the tarot, entitled *Tarot for Today: Instantaneous Insights and Effective Affirmations,* which is scheduled for release in early 2000.

Patricia is also the author of *The Wheel of Destiny: The Tarot Reveals Your Master Plan* and two plays, *Sidney* and *Love is Contagious. The Recycling of Rosalie* is her first novel.

Visit the web site of Patricia McLaine—International Psychic
www.ucando.com/p/psychicmclaine.html
PsychicPM@aol.com
800-816-3556